# Into a Long Ago Future

## A Collection of Short Fiction

*by*

Jodi Lee

# Into a Long Ago Future

**A Collection of Short Fiction**
*by*
**Jodi Lee**

Jodi Lee – http://www.jodilee.ca

# Also by the Author

**Eternity Series:**
*Fire & Ice*
*Beyond the Veil*

**Creating New Pagan Family Traditions:**
*Yule*
*Imbolc*

**Releasing in 2012:**

*Eternity Series:*
Betrayal
Outworld
Damned
Eternal

*Creating New Pagan Family Traditions:*
Ostara
Beltaine
Litha
Lughnasadh
Mabon
Samhain
Esbats

# Publication Credits

The Lion Roared -
> *Tales from the Moonlit Path* 2006
> *Tainted Anthology* 2008
> *The Monsters Next Door - Road Trip* 2009

Thirsty -
> *Night to Dawn #11* 2007
> *Horrorology Anthology* 2011

Black and White -
> *Nocturnal Ooze* 2007

Clipped -
> *Fried! Fast Food, Slow Deaths Anthology* 2007

Days, Hours, Minutes, Seconds -
> *Parasitic Thoughts Anthology* 2008

It Never Lasts Forever -
> *Fifty-Two Stitches, Webzine & Anthology* 2009

The Legless Ones -
> *The Black Garden Anthology* 2009

Down the Street -

Through New Bedlam -

The Institute -

On the Road -
> *The New Bedlam Project* 2009

Doe Clock Truck -

New Bedlam -
> *The New Bedlam Project* 2010

My Beautiful Boy -
> *War of the Worlds: Frontlines Anthology* 2010

Ring a Ring a Rosie -
> *Necrotic Tissue #9* 2010

Chopped Up Pop -
> *Necrotic Tissue #11* 2010

# Acknowledgments

I could never have done this little project if my editor, Melanie Choly, hadn't taken it over and whipped it into shape. She was sent a bunch of loose files, part of a story on a handful of torn and crumpled notebook pages, and even managed to find a story I'd thought lost to the ages. And she turned it into this.

I owe you, Mel. Still, forever, and always. I promise Morpheus will bless you, eventually.

I also want to acknowledge the support and friendship of Tug, Mr. Sir, and the forever wonderful Werepig. Together, we were four Musketeers, battling insomnia with laughter and snark wherever we rode.

# Dedication

For Rhiannon & Carrie, who put up with late dinners, lots of chores and a cranky mom who stays up all night. Love you!

For the members of Glas Celli, who put up with lack of communication, absentmindedness, and distraction ...
You are the best family I could ever have wished for.

And as always, for Gran & Gramps. *Thank you.*

# Contents

# Down the Street

She's lived in New Bedlam all her life, this starry-eyed girl who sees nothing but a life outside the little town of horrors. She doesn't want to wash their laundry anymore, she doesn't want to see and feel their sins as the blood drips and flows away from her white linens.

She wants, more than anything, to leave. Someday, a stranger will come down the highway, turn into town and take her away with him. Someday, she'll stand on a stage and smile and sing and the people will love her.

She's lived in New Bedlam all her life, this exhausted soccer-mother who has long since given up on her dreams of stage and fame. Never will she stand before the lights too bright to see beyond, never will she feel their heat upon her face.

Still she hopes to see the end of the town she's forever lived in. There will be no more blood. There will be no more bones. There will be no more stories of late-night carousing with the monster under the bed or the boogeyman in the closet.

There will be no more stories, period.

And the monsters will sleep.

And the people will sleep.

And the streets of New Bedlam will finally, *finally* be safe for anyone to walk.

She's lived in New Bedlam all her life, and as she rests her graying head upon her pillow for the last time, she begs Morpheus for just one dance before the dawn.

# Trip 'em

You want to survive a zombie apocalypse, you need a plan.

You need to *think*; one morning, everyone'll wake up to news reports that the dead have begun walking, which will lead into the cries of the dead biting, which will lead to the inevitable panic and scramble for guns and supplies. And then of course the fires, the looting, the general lack of sanity until finally, martial law.

That martial law, that's gonna be the fun times.

Here's how you could avoid all of that, just by being prepared ahead of time.

Cases of water are darn cheap, and even though it'll grate your nerves to pay for something that came out of a tap somewhere else, until you get a well working, you'll need drinking water. Remember, buying water in bulk ain't the only thing you can do; every heavily populated area has a wholesaler club of some sort, you know—like Costco. Get a membership, start picking up a case or two here and there. If you're really mad on getting things ready, do it all at once.

*No one* questions a survivalist with a credit card and a trolley loaded down with cases of non-perishables and water at Costco. Trust me. They may look at you, but they'll glance away fast so they don't make eye contact by accident. Just smile big if they do stare.

Freaks out the non-believers if you're not only preparing for the end of the world, but you're *happy* to do so.

So, then you're thinkin', *what all would I need to pick up in order to survive through at least the first six months?* Well, let's tick off a basic list; you'll have to work out quantities depending on who you'll be keeping with you to the end.

You'd need your water, freeze-dried veggies and fruits, canned goods like meats and beans and chili and soups. I know it sounds bulky, but toilet paper. You don't want to wipe your ass with poison ivy by accident, do you?

Let's see. Jerky, all kinds of jerky. That stuff'd make it through the next nuclear war, so it'd do ya good. Believe it or not, you can boil it up in water to create soups and stews, too.

Those squiggly noodles the college kids are all ravin' about all the time. What d'ya call 'em... Ramon noodles.

What? Oh. *Ramen*. Ramon, Ramen, all the same to me.

Macaroni and cheese from a box. Every little kid's favorite, right? Bet they'd never dream they'd be livin' off it when they grew up.

Drugs. Gotta stock up on drugs, and *early*, too, because once the zombies really hit, every store is gonna be either inaccessible or looted, probably cleaned right out. Grab your ibuprofen and your acetaminophen and anti-bacterial soaps and what nots. Can't forget the air freshener and the lady-goods. Of course, you're needing blankets for sleeping and back-packs for all this stuff.

Now I bet you're wondering why I included air freshener and 'lady-goods.' Air freshener for the camp because you'll be eating a lot of beans and frankly, you'll stink. 'Lady-goods' are on the list because you're gonna end up with at least one woman with you, and she's likely going to need them. Even if you didn't plan on or don't end up with a female in your group, have some on hand anyway; they make excellent field bandages in an emergency. If you get the kind with a scent, it'll keep the blood smell from attracting the attention of the wandering horde.

This next bit of advice would probably hurt your sensibilities a bit, but you need to man up and grow a pair if you're gonna come out the other end of this still breathing.

You need to find *someone*. Someone older, or maybe just less physically capable. Maybe even more than one. Make friends. Don't tell me you don't know where I'm going with this, I know you know. If you don't think you could do what I'm about to tell you, take the sucky out of your mouth and stop squalling for your mama's teat.

A whole new kind of critter wants that now.

What? Yeah, I went there. Ain't such a pretty picture, huh? You're goddamn right it ain't. Now, are you ready to do what needs to be done to save your own skin? No pun intended.

See the way I figure it, as long as you're faster and stronger than at least one person in your group, you're doin' good. And if you're not, well buddy, just *trip 'em*. That's all ya gotta do. Stick out your leg and let the next guy tumble over it. Unless he's a gymnastic genius, he's not gonna get up fast enough to keep from being a horde's midnight snack.

One thing though, you'd need to make damn sure that it looked like an accident, or *you'll* be the next one eating a dirt sandwich. Trust me.

Ah, hell, I'm getting ahead of myself, ain't I?

The other thing you need to do, once you have a shitload of supplies, is scatter them around a bit, have a few hidey-holes around. You'll have to make sure they're well secured, or some idiotic, Dawn of the Dead-watching freak could find your stash and take it down to the mall.

*No.* Ya saw how that turned out, right? A steel-reinforced room, a good solid combination lock doubled up with a hella-strong padlock. Yeah, that's the way to go.

See now, it ain't gonna matter how secure your hideout is, they're gonna get in eventually. If Hollywood has taught us nothing else, it's that zombies *always* get fed, and the food *always* needs to find new places to hide out.

You should've scouted out three, maybe four, places to hang your hat when the time come. I suggest you stay out of basements, actually. Unless you've got access to some super-secret, mega-secure bomb-shelter under here… just stay out of places that are easily accessible, but hard to get out of in a pinch.

Find all your spots, get your rooms done up and get to storing your necessities, you'd be nearly set. Come to think of it, it probably wouldn't hurt to get one of them camper toilets for each of your hidey-holes. No running water and such'll make it a bitch to… eliminate.

Quit smirkin'. I know I'm cruder than the oil ol' Jed Clampett shot out the ground, but I still have sense enough to keep some things delicate.

Last thing, guns. *Lots* of guns, and that means lots of ammo. Lots of ammo means an ammo belt to keep it secure.

That's where you went wrong, I think.

I think *you* should have tripped that old guy that got his foot out in front of you. If you'd have just done what I've told you, I wouldn't be ready to start gnawin' on your innards.

Oh, stop your bawlin', boy. In an hour or so, ain't none of this gonna matter to you anyhow.

Bet you wish you'd tripped 'em, huh?

# Supernova

There was a huge blank spot in the night sky where she knew there had been stars the night before.

*Doesn't it take seven years for anything out* there *to be visible* here? she thought to herself. *Maybe I should call Brandt and let him know.* Brandt, the boss-man at the astronomy lab where no one had ever found anything of importance. Brandt, the spoiled heir to millions with his own astronomy lab as a toy. Jeanie's hand reached out to the red phone on the desk. *I just don't want to be on the end of his stick if he's drunk again.* She glanced at the screen again, and then moved her hand away from the phone.

For all she knew, it was an anomaly in the software. *It just wasn't a big deal.*

"It's not your fault... you know that, right Dec? Anyone could have made that mistake. That's why they put *you* there to do it. They needed someone they could blame in the end." Roos spoke quietly, without looking at the man piloting the ship. The silence from his companion annoyed him, and he sighed. "If you hadn't been making eyes at the Grand Sindai's daughter, they would have chosen Taw, and we'd all be on the Scart now, sipping wine and nibbling craksin pir."

"I thought you said it wasn't my fault." Dec responded.

"All right, Dec, I was wrong. It *is* your fault. Is that what you want to hear? The thing about the Grand Sindai's daughter is true, the rest... as I said. Anyone could have made that mistake. Taw would have been a better choice though."

*"Dec, we've cleared the rim. We can shut the generator down and just coast on the blast wave for a while."*

Roos winced at the voice that interrupted his rant, and turned away from the shield. Spinning his seat around, he rose and left the deck, slamming the connecting door on his way through.

"That's fine, Jessa. It's not like we're in a hurry to get anywhere."

"*Is Roos with you? He's sup*—" Static broke the connection and Dec reached over to snap the intercom off. He was not going to get involved in the marital spats of his friends and co-escapees. Not when they needed each other more than ever. Not ever, for that matter.

He stared out at the mass of sparkly optimism in front of him; each star and planetary system meant a possible match to their biological needs. *So many to look through, so little time.* They only had enough fuel to travel to the next sector, but if Jessa was right and they could ride the wave for a while, they'd be okay. *Maybe.*

Dec rubbed his forehead. He hated that he'd put his friends into this situation, but the Sindai court *had* asked him to chose twenty people he could make use of. Rather than leave his friends behind he'd chosen them, all eighteen of them. His sister - nineteen - had declined the order, opting instead to flee with her Sindai lover. The last one, Dai-Tan, was sleeping in his quarters.

The court had fussed, but could not refuse his request. Had they any forethought at all, they would have known he'd take the Grand Sindai's daughter with him.

He was not interested in mating with the girl, he was only interested in getting the map on her shoulder analyzed and perhaps go treasure hunting. Unfortunately, Dai-Tan was not taking well to travel, and was quite ill. Her color had lightened, and the hair had begun to fall from her head. The shadows under her eyes suggested she didn't have much time left.

Dec cared little if the girl died on their trip. He'd simply hack the skin from her body, and eject the remains from the ship. She may have thought he was in love with her, but he couldn't bring himself to actually mate with a Sindai. He wanted someone like him.

Pushing a button on the console, Dec brought up a ghost-image on the shield in front of him. The black emptiness where Sindaise-Prime had been only days ago tugged at his heart. He was not of the Sindaise race, but had lived among those on Sindaise-Prime all his life. He'd been born there, created by recombining scattered bio-material gleaned from rogue debris bearing the marker O-R-B-I-T-E; a *Geno*. Dec had actually seen the debris pile at the station, and thought it looked as though it was from one very large ship. The Sindaise begged to differ, and he was punished for his insolence.

Sindaise-Prime had been his home, just as it was theirs. He hadn't meant to destroy it performing the one task they'd given him to prepare him for citizenship.

Jeanie cleaned her station before preparing the coffee, pushing the ball of anger down deep where it wouldn't surface for at least another day. Not once had Brandt cleaned away his crap before she started her shift.

Brandt had circled the anomaly on the screen. Not on a print out, but on the computer screen itself. "Asshole!" she mumbled as she tried to clean it off. Naturally the man was too dense to use a washable marker.

"What was that, Jeanie?" he whispered close to her ear, causing her to jump.

"Nothing, Brandt. I stubbed my toe when I shifted over here."

"All right then. I want you to keep your eye on that spot, Jeanie." His huge sausage finger pointed to the circle on the screen. "All right then, I'm out of here. I have a date. I don't want to be disturbed, so just print anything out and leave it here. I'll see it in the morning."

"*All right then*, right back atcha, you officious little prick." Jeanie whispered as he exited the office.

He was gone only fifteen minutes when the red light on the wall snapped on, and the alarm sounded.

In his dream, Dec stood on the platform, his arms raised to the skies, armed with an intricately carved metal in one hand, and his short-blade in the other. The bowl before him was filled with fire, the blue and green flames dancing like lovers in the moonlight. The crowds around him were silent in their awe.

"I call you down, great Tahsinh. Come, give your people your blessings!" Dec's voice carried well over the crowd, and each person below echoed his call.

Thunder sounded, although the sky was clear and the stars shone brightly. Dec continued with his ritual, not taking heed of the warning from the gods. Ignoring the murmuring crowd.

"Tahsinh, come now, come forth, I demand you!"

Dec lost his footing as the ground beneath the platform bulged, then sank slightly. The Sindaise and the Genos below screamed as the bowl of fire fell forward, raining sparks and coals over their naked bodies. The Genos could stand having some damage to their outer skin, but the Sindaise burned easily and many now lay dying, oozing their yellowish fluids onto the ground. The Genos spilled their fluids just as easily, but theirs was red and thick, soon drying over the wounds, sealing them—even if burned.

Dec tried to maintain his footing but soon fell forward into the remaining crowd, now mostly Genos. They carried him across the compound to more solid ground, away from the destruction at the platform.

It wasn't long before a Sindaise hover came to collect the Genos and take them away. Something in Dec's ritual had gone terribly wrong, and they were now all under arrest. Genos were not allowed to practice the Sindaise religion. No Geno had ever performed an *evokemeneal* before, the prophecy warned of the results. As fire exploded from under the feet of the citizens of Sindaise-Prime, they realized prophecy spoke true. *Should any Geno insult the gods of Sindai, ever shall they and the Sindaise suffer.* Dec's voice woke him, and he lay shivering in the dark.

The Sindaise-Prime system sun went supernova a week after Dec and his crew had been exiled from Sindaise-Seco. A day later, when the blast wave hit Sindaise-Seco, it too, was obliterated. The Sindai, except for those aboard Dec's ship and the escape pods, were no more.


Jeanie tracked the movement from the black spot without printing it, without analyzing it. She simply watched. Brandt hadn't wanted to be disturbed and the disgusting mass of jelly could just suck it up and take it like the man he was.

*He'll cry when he realizes I get this discovery, not him.* Jeanie was taking particular delight in that, more so than having made a discovery at all. She'd already called it in to National, and SETI. SETI was covering it under her ID number, and National had already taken down her information. The only accolades Brandt would be given was that his lab would be named. She laughed.

The phone jangled beside her. Checking the little red light on the red phone first, she then picked up the receiver on the black one. "Hello, Brandt Astronomy, Jeanie speaking. How can I help you?"

"Jeanie, Steve here. We have some news for you." Steve was a researcher at SETI, currently head of the research department. He and Jeanie had attended college together, vowing to be the first to make alien contact. Instead, they'd made first contact with each other.

"What is it, Steve? Is it debris?" Jeanie tried not to sound let down; with her luck, she just had a feeling it would be debris.

"No. Is Brandt there?" Steve was trying to sound casual, but something in his voice led Jeanie to believe he was about to snap like a twig.

"Absolutely not. He's away on a date. Don't laugh, I've met her. What is it Steve?"

"No, I can't do that until you tell me if the machine under the desk is running."

Jeanie knew Steve meant the phone-recorder. "Nope. I shut it off before I called you to begin with. Think I really want him to know about this until it hits the papers? Besides, I think he wanks to our conversations."

"Jesus, Jeanie!"

"All right, all right. Sorry. Go ahead." She had a notepad beside her, ready to write down anything he might say.

"It's holding a steady course, and it's slowing down, Jeanie. By dawn the ship will be at the moon and by four we'll be having tea with whatever is on it."

She couldn't respond; her hand was covering her mouth and she was shaking uncontrollably. *Contact!*

Dec put Roos in charge of navigating the system they'd arrived in. He'd been here before, although only on the outer edges, skirting the planet they knew had life on it. The Sindai council did not want to be discovered creeping around in someone's backyard.

Dec retired to his cabin, checking in on Dai-Tan. Her eyes were slightly open, the deep purple irises clouded over. Her cheeks had sunken in, making her seem even more skeletal than normal. He poked her, gently at first then with more force when she didn't respond. Finally he put his hand down on her chest, and realized she wasn't breathing at all.

Sighing, he began the task of removing the map and disposing of her body.

Roos tried to hide the ship behind a small satellite orbiting the planet they'd been warned away from. When the communications light came on, he knew he'd been unsuccessful. He rose to alert Dec, but ran right into the larger man standing in the doorway. Over the beeping from the console, they spoke.

"She's dead."

"They found us."

They stared at each other. Roos wanted to believe Dec hadn't deliberately killed Dai-Tan, but had discovered in the last weeks that he didn't really know his friend all that well. It wasn't just that they were of different races, but more that Dec had become so withdrawn and moody over the accident on Sindaise-Prime. The Dec he knew wouldn't have cared this much.

Dec didn't want to believe Roos had deliberately let themselves be found, but he was finding it hard to trust the Sindai, and since Roos was basically the senior Sindai on the ship, Dec was trusting him the least. Growing up together they'd never been apart, never argued. Now though... the race issue was coming up more and more often.

"I tried getting the ship behind the satellite in time, but they have many more scanners now. Many, *many* more. I thought you'd want to do the contact, since the ship is yours." Roos offered a smile, which Dec ignored. "Have you disposed of Dai-Tan's body?"

That simple comment earned Roos a glare Dec knew he'd never seen focused on him. The smile faded as Dec shoved past and sat at the console. "Take this down to Jessa and see what she can make of it now that it's off Dai-Tan." His outstretched hand held a still-damp swatch of Dai-Tan's skin, marked with darker pigment that outlined the map.

Anger flashed on Roos' face, showing he his anger at the desecration performed on one of his own and disgust at having to touch the flap of skin. Taking the map between his finger and thumb, he turned and left the deck.

Dec sat with his fingers in his mouth as he often did when tense. The taste of her blood lingered and caused his heart to jump.

Shrugging it off, he contemplated their situation. Contact protocol was written specifically for this planet. He'd read it early on in flight school. He knew what to do. Pushing certain keys on the board in front of him, a detailed grouping of mathematical equations were broadcast from the ship. The equations were basically a simpler way of saying *'hello.'*

Resting his head in his hands, he allowed a moment of grief to wash over him. Roos would laugh if he were to come in now, unannounced. Dec wiped at the fluids leaking from his eyes.

The com crackled with static, and he stared at it. A high-pitched, probably female voice broke through the interference.

*"This is Jeanie Scott at Brandt Lab in Arnelle. I send greetings on behalf of the Commonwealth of Independent Countries. Welcome."*

Dec understood every word she said. He'd heard that language before, they taught it in flight school. He wondered if she'd be surprised when she heard his voice, and cleared his throat before reaching out to push another button.

"This is Dec, formerly of Sindaise-Prime. Exiled for breaking law and planetary destruction. I am Geno, the rest on board are Sindaise."

More static was the only response.

Jeanie stood fidgeting with her skirt and hair. Steve kept poking her, whispering that she was fine, that she needed to pay attention. She was about to meet the now-infamous Dec. The Sindaise refused to exit the ship, but Dec had come willingly, surprising the Commonwealth President. Apparently, Dec was equally as surprised that the Sindaise would not descend from their ship, and gave up trying to convince them to come down.

Finally, it was Jeanie's turn. Dec held out his hand— remarkably warm flesh with four fingers and a thumb—embraced hers and shook it gently before releasing it. When she looked into his eyes, she saw irises of deepest blue.

On July 18th 2012, in preparation of the Apocalypse prophecies revolving around the Mayan Calendar completion the following December, the DNA of the finest scholars and athletes of the 21st century had been placed aboard the Oribter Module Flight 616 before it was launched into space.

# Jogger

Andrew stopped cold on the hiking trail, mid-stride.

He had no idea there was a woman jogging behind until she ran right into him, knocking him over and falling on top of him, her legs splaying out across his back.

From their positions, it was difficult to extricate themselves without losing any and all dignity. After several moments of tussling around to get a footing, she finally dug her elbow into the soft tissue between his shoulder blades, to push herself up and off. She glared down at him as she dusted herself off.

"Just what the hell did you think you were doing, asshole? No one—*no one*—stops in the middle of the path without stepping aside," she ranted at him, her breath coming hard and fast.

"I had no choice but to stop. Can't you see that?" he replied, rolling to his side and pointing ahead a bare few inches.

There on the path, seeming to glitter in the leaf-filtered sunlight, was an eye. Small and drying out, but with the brightest blue iris he'd ever seen. Just the eyeball and a bit of stalk. No blood.

"Oh Jesus! What the hell?" she squealed as she covered her mouth. "What the *fuck?*" The woman spun on her heel and bent into the bushes next to the path.

Between the sight of the eye, and her wet retching sounds, Andrew nearly joined her.

Getting to his feet, he dug in his pack for a cloth and held it out for her when she faced him again. Nodding gratefully, the woman wet it with water from her bottle and wiped her mouth, eyes and neck.

"I don't know why or what or how. All I know is, there it sits." Andrew reached into a side pocket of his pack and pulled out his cell phone. With shaking fingers, he pressed the emergency quick-dial button and hoped for the best. He didn't always get the greatest reception this far into the park, despite his signal booster and the tower at the ranger station.

"911, please state the nature of your emergency." A harassed sounding, androgynous voice came from the phone.

Suddenly Andrew had no idea how to go about explaining the situation.

"Yeah, um, hi. I'm hiking in Rider Mountain Park, on trail sixty-three. I think I just passed the mile ten marker…" he glanced at the woman to see if she had noticed on her way down; she nodded so he turned back to the call. "Yeah, it's mile ten. There's an eye on the path."

Silence from Andrew for a moment as he listened to the call handler.

"I'm not joking around. It's an eye, it's *sans* owner and it's blue." *Like telling them the color of the iris is going to help,* he thought to himself. He glanced back to his erstwhile companion, who was looking everywhere and anywhere, but at the eye. "No, I'm not alone. A jogger came along behind me, she's still here as well… how the hell am I supposed to know? Just a minute." Andrew turned to the woman, and passed her the phone. "911 wants your name."

Dealing with an overworked emergency services worker wasn't what he needed to do, he needed to take a deep breath and center himself, get calm, get happy. Andrew's resolve waned as a vision of someone coming along, picking the eye up and putting it into an empty socket in their own skull came to him, and he nearly stepped on the offending eyeball as he lurched away. He just managed to pull his foot back, feeling like the orb was watching him from dirty path; he barely had time to find a bush of his own to retch into. After a moment, he straightened and wiped his mouth with his jacket sleeve.

"Yes, I understand. I'll give him the phone and let you finish up with him." She passed the phone back to Andrew, and after a moment gave him his cloth back, rinsed and ready to wipe his own face. She smiled sympathetically as he thanked her.

"They'll be here in a half hour. We've been asked to stay here so they can speak to us, and help them find it. It's not like the thing is going to get up and walk away though." He shuddered, turning away from the eye's glare.

"I'm Andrew, by the way." He held his hand out, and she took it.

"I'm Stephanie. I guess I'm pleased to meet you."

Her smile was brilliant. *Under other circumstances,* Andrew thought, *I'd have no problems falling in love with her.* He shook his head, wondering where that thought had surfaced from.

They made themselves as comfortable as they could, sitting in the sparse grass on the opposite side of the path from their respective messes. They talked a little about the park, the city and their jobs as they waited. It seemed to be much longer than a half hour later when Andrew checked his watch; he was right, it had been an hour.

"They're late. Think we should call again?" he asked Stephanie. After catching a brief nod out of the corner of his eye, he dialed 911 again. The line was busy and stayed that way for some time, and finally he gave up. Angrily sliding his phone shut and jamming it into his pocket.

The tension was mounting again, and after another half hour the pair of them threatened to walk away, leaving the eye behind them.

"Isn't that the same as leaving the scene of an accident though? I mean, we gave them our names. They could track us down," Stephanie commented. Andrew thought she seemed pretty sure they'd get into trouble if they left.

"At this point I don't care. They can check the records on my cell—I've been calling. It's now…" Andrew glanced at his watch again. "10 AM and they were supposed to be here at 8:30. I'm just glad I'm not working today. I'd be fired for being this late, under normal circumstances."

Stephanie nodded. She didn't need to tell him she was late for work; she'd been getting more and more fidgety as time passed. "Could I borrow your phone for a moment? I really should call in so they know where I am. I don't necessarily have to be there, but I should let them know I'm okay."

Andrew handed her the phone, his brow wrinkling as he contemplated her words. *Who doesn't need to go in to work, unless they work from home or owned their own business?*

He watched her shift her weight from one leg to the other as she spoke to someone on the other end of the call, her tight bicycle shorts showing off every curve as she did so. Despite the situation, despite the anxiety he was feeling, Andrew felt himself getting aroused.

Or at least *interested*, and that in itself hadn't happened in a very long time. Again, he couldn't figure out why he would be having such ideas in the situation he found himself in.

She walked back to him, smiling, and again he found himself thinking he could fall in love with her. Involuntarily, his eyes slipped lower and he watched the rise and fall of her chest with each step she took. Glancing upwards again, Andrew realized he'd been caught and grinned apologetically.

"Like what you see, Andrew?" she asked, sitting down beside him again. When she was settled, she looked him in the eye, quite openly. Obviously, she expected a truthful answer and he found he couldn't lie.

"Yes. I do." He nodded, as if to emphasize the point. "I'm sorry, it... it's been a long time. My wife, Nora... she died six months ago." Andrew glanced away for a moment, hiding his emotions. "She was sick for some time before that. I'm sorry if I offended you, Stephanie. I've never... you are an extraordinarily beautiful woman."

Stephanie brushed the hair from her forehead, leaned in and put the tip of her forefinger on Andrew's chin. An almost intangible electric shock radiated from that contact point, along his jaw-line and up, directly into his temple. He was forced to look at her again. *That was most definitely not static electricity...*

She placed her lips against his, applying the lightest of pressure. She kept her eyes open, and so she saw his reaction. Andrew had closed his eyes, and given himself over to her. *Good. This is almost too easy.*

She let her tongue slide between his lips and from there she explored his mouth. As she did so, she closed her fist around his cell phone, muffling the beep as she turned it off.

Carefully, not breaking the physical contact between them, she leaned in further and rolled slightly to the side. Within moments, she could feel Andrew's passion had grown so he wouldn't be noticing anything outside of their own small embrace.

She pulled him over on top of her, sliding her arms around him. Andrew ran a hand along her side, under her tank top. He didn't seem surprised to find her bra-less under it; his fingers never faltered in their exploration. She moved her hips beneath him, lowering her shorts, her hands then swiftly taking care of his zipper, and shoving his pants down over his hips. Still without breaking their kiss, she pulled him into her…

Andrew felt as though he were floating on a whole oceans worth of waves, each one holding more pleasure than the last. It had been so long and he was so completely, utterly, *strangely* turned on that it wasn't any time at all before he felt the first warnings of orgasm.

Stephanie moved under him suddenly and then he was on his back, feeling something move and pop under his shoulder, but far too deep into his own mounting climax to care what it was.

He opened his eyes just as he began to come, feeling his semen exploding into Stephanie.

At the last convulsive twitches, her face began to change.

She was no longer beautiful, in fact she wasn't even pretty. Her skin had become a sleek, shiny grey and instead of her beautiful, full lips, she had some kind of sucker; the kind he imagined a leech would have. Above that, her nose and eyes had melted together, forming a cluster of tiny dark orbs.

His scream was cut off by the sucker of her mouth.

When she pulled back, his lips and a large part of his tongue were gone. Regardless, Andrew continued to try and scream.

She rose, picking him up as though he were nothing more than a sack of flour, and standing him roughly on his feet. Moaning, he looked down as she pointed to the ground where they had only moments before been fucking like bunnies.

*They'd been on the path.*

When she'd rolled them to ride his cock, he'd rolled *over* the eyeball; that was the squishy pop he'd felt against his back. As he stood, mind trapped within the sheer terror of it all, Stephanie grabbed a fistful of his hair and ripped his head back.

She slid a claw across and under the lower eyelid of her captive's right eye, severing the anchors holding it in his skull, sliding it out onto her hand. Stuffing the orb into her mouth, she repeated the action on the other side—all while chewing happily.

Andrew's odd, gurgling screams were heard by no one.

At that time of morning, this area of the park was always abandoned. She rolled Andrew's left eye in her hand as she thought perhaps she'd gone too far in destroying the eye on the path; rather than having a full meal, she'd have to use part of it as bait again.

Popping the eye into her mouth, she gobbled it down while deciding which part to use.

He had begun to try and scream again, the garbled sounds wearing on her nerves. Grabbing either side of his head, she spun it to the side, snapping his neck.

Andrew Walton existed no longer, his voice cut short.

She realized his pants were still around his ankles, providing her easy access to the perfect bait. She was smiling as she tore his penis from his crotch and dropped it at her feet.

Her hunger was only slightly abated—but she would eat well tonight.

# Spilt

you come to me
always alive
always real
always physical

i hear your voice
i see your smile
i feel your mind
i am inside

the box won't close
the mist never fades
the blood's been spilt
on the hilt of the blade

hands cold, eyes shining
i pull the knife free
to remember you
i give it a twist

will you feel this?
someday, somehow
you will
look back and see

what you've done to me

# Faith and Lies

"By that time the lie had spread so far and wide that everyone believed it to be the truth. It was too late."

The young man on the couch shrugged and sighed. "We really couldn't do anything. Jud tried for a day or so, then took the money we'd been paid—all of it, mind you—and buggered off. You know they found him hanging from that tree, right? The one they ended up naming after him, sick bastards."

A bespectacled older man with a graying beard sat with his legs crossed and a notepad on his knee. He nodded, indicating the young man, Nate, should continue. He wondered how this story would tie in to Nate's belief that he was a vampire.

"Okay, well, Pete was found wandering about in the desert. Apparently *his* guilt didn't run as deep as Jud's, as deep as mine. He'd gathered up the faithful, had them following him just as they'd followed…"

The doctor noticed Nate's quick glance, checking to see if he was paying attention.

"…as they'd followed Joshua. He had them convinced that Joshua had come back from the dead. Can you believe that? I mean shit! Granted, none of them saw the incident, but how can they swallow that kind of story without thinking about it? Without questioning?" Nate thumped the pillow on the couch before putting his head down.

When the younger man threw his arm over his eyes, the therapist knew he was finally getting close to a breakthrough. He'd heard all of the strange stories so many times before, but never had the younger man been so emotional. A sly tilt of his head brought the hidden camera into view. "Go on Nate, please continue."

A heavy sigh was the only response. They had time; there was still twenty minutes left in the session.

Finally, Nate sat up again. His damp eyes gave away the tears he'd tried to hide. "Doc, you know how it is, man. It's hard talking about all of this. It means a lot you can see me in the evenings though. Not many docs would do that." A slow grin spread over Nate's face—even reaching his eyes this time.

The older man felt that twinge in his chest again. Guilt, wrapped in the fear that if Nate were to ever make a move on him, he'd gladly go, give in to that forbidden pleasure.

Nate was beautiful.

"Okay, Doc, stop giving me that look. I don't know what happened to the rest of them. I've seen them since, over the years. Our eyes will catch each other across a crowd or something. We're polite to each other now, but we're not friendly. Even Maggie isn't as sociable anymore, and she was the most open one of us, if you know what I mean. She was gracious and damn *good* at being responsive." He was grinning, a young man's smile meant to show he remembered a lost love.

"We all just went our separate ways. There wasn't much to stick around for after Joshua. I know you think *I'm* beautiful Doc, but you shoulda seen *him!*"

The doctor hoped his flinch hadn't been noticed. Suddenly, he felt very uncomfortable being alone with the younger man.

"He had everything a woman could want, and Maggie wanted him. Oh, she was with all of us at some point or other, but it was him she wanted. Joshua. I think she only slept with me because I looked like him, a little. He wanted her too—finally giving in to her charms close to the end there. Now that was a wedding!" Nate glanced up to meet the doctor's eyes. "You knew they were married right? I mentioned that before?"

The doctor shook his head. "No, Nate, we've never quite made it that far. Please… continue."

"Maggie spent the wedding night with him, and the next night. Then, when they came to get him and take him away—she disappeared. I often used to wonder if she'd had something to do with Jud's plan, but she didn't. I know that now.

"Joshua held out as long as he could, to give us all time to get out, get to safety. Almost all of us did, except Jud. He couldn't escape his own mind. Maggie, Simon, Pete and me, we all got away. The rest, well. I know they got out, like I said, I've seen them. But they weren't directly in on it. It was Simon that came to me with the plan. *Jud's* plan.

Pete overheard us and wanted in. Maggie knew about it, but only later, after they'd already taken Joshua away… she was too scared to try and help then though." Nate put his elbows on his knees, burying his face in his hands.

"I watched the trial, I watched as people who claimed to love him turned on him. I watched as even the judge stepped down because he'd believed in Joshua's innocence. It was Jud's damned story that got Joshua into that mess, and I just couldn't say anything to stop the shit that happened. Jud deserved to die, to die the way he did. Personally, I'd have flayed him before I hung him on that tree with his guts hanging out. I'd have flayed him alive."

There was no noticeable reaction from the doctor. Inside though, the man was nearly screaming. He'd found himself beginning to believe Nate's delusions. Beginning to believe Nate was dangerous.

"It was always love, acceptance and respect with Joshua. He loved everyone, and pretty much everyone loved him. It was Jud's damn lies that got Joshua killed, and *my* damn face that got him martyred. Joshua was dead. The dead don't get up and walk."

The doctor couldn't repress the twitching of his hand now.

Nate glanced at him again, smiling serenely. "Well, not *all* dead get up and walk." His smile grew larger, and for the first time, the doctor saw a flash of white teeth. Unconsciously, his eyes moved to the spot where the camera sat tucked into the fake book on the shelf.

"Now, Doc, did you really think I couldn't hear that stupid thing? I've known all along you've been recording our sessions. Although, I believe this is the first time you've used the video camera."

The older man scrambled to his feet, nearly knocking the chair over in his haste. Nate was faster and had the doctor by his neck before he'd even found his feet. Putting a slender finger against the man's lips, he shushed the scream that was building.

"You don't want to do that Doc. Nope, you really don't want to do that. I'm not finished talking yet." Nate released him, and the older man sat with a thump. "Good. You sit there and listen, and we'll let the camera keep running. How's that?"

Nate went to the window and waved. "You get to meet someone now, Doc. Someone very important to me." He moved to the door; upon opening it, a young woman of exquisite beauty entered.

Long, rich-chocolate colored hair flowed in waves over her shoulders and down to the middle of her back. Eyes the color of sapphires flashed with nearly neon qualities as she smiled at the old man. Unnaturally bright white teeth seemed to glow in the gloomy dusk of the room.

"Doc, I want you to meet Maggie. Maggie, this is the man that's been helping me sort through things. He's going to help both of us now." Nate grinned widely, this time showing all of his teeth.

Maggie came around to stand in front of the doctor. She smiled gently down at him, showing her delicately pointed canines. He whimpered.

"They paid us—Jud, Pete, Simon and me—to play a little game with the folks following Joshua. Jud was to point him out, Pete was to confuse people, Simon was to tell the story that he was really alive; the reality was he was very dead. As long as none of us went back on our stories and did what we'd been paid to do—we'd have been fine. But Jud had to go and kill himself. He damned the rest of us, *all* of us, to this. To what we are now." Nate sighed, and turned to Maggie.

She took Nate's hand and dug her nails deep into his palm. Tiny drops of blood ran down his fingers to spatter the floor. Her sing-song voice continued the story as she and Nate sat on the couch.

"I loved Joshua with all of my heart and soul. He rescued me. He took me from the squalor and despair I'd been forced into. What I was, that was how he met me; I'd slept with each of his men and they spoke of me.

"When I met Nate, I thought I was in love. When he introduced me to Joshua I *knew* I was in love—wildly in love, but with Joshua." Maggie's slender arms crossed over her chest. "When he touched me, I was lost to him forever. When we married, I was thrilled to have a real life with a man I loved. Jud destroyed all of that. Jud was the reason Joshua was killed—Jud and his thirty pieces of silver. The others, they didn't know everything and Jud convinced them it was all a joke, all a game. It would be okay, they'd release Joshua and we'd all go on as before." Maggie picked up the Bible that sat on the corner table beside the couch, and tapped her finger nail on the cover.

"You know that's not what happened. You know what happened to Joshua. They tried him, convicted him and crucified him. Nate and the others didn't come in to it until after. When Jud found out what I'd done—what Joshua and I had done together—he realized his errors. He realized he'd wronged all of us, but *especially* Joshua. He killed himself, hung himself from that stupid tree," she smiled as she took a calming breath.

"And now we need your help. We've waited an eternity."

"Why me?" the old man whispered. Tears flowed freely from his eyes and ran down, dripping from his jowls and chin. "What can I do?"

Maggie smiled serenely. A glow seemed to emanate from her face. "Nate found you for me, Doc. You see, Joshua and I had two nights together before they took him and killed him. Two nights, and we'd planned our wedding well. We'd planned it to coincide with my most fertile time. I am pregnant."

"I don't understand. I'm not an OB-GYN. I'm a psychiatrist." He turned to face Nate again.

"Jud had two sisters and a brother. His sisters were killed during a raid of the encampment they were in. His brother—he was a bit of a no-good. He disappeared about a year after Jud was found dead. He did have children however, and one of those spoke of her uncle hanging from the tree." Nate replied smoothly. "And those children have had children. One night's drunken chatter, and the family was reasonably easy to track. We couldn't get close enough until now, to make sure. You, Doc, are Jud's descendant, if through a sibling rather than himself."

"Well, it wouldn't have been Jud anyway. He was unable to…" Maggie started, but was stopped short by a glare from Nate.

"How can I… but I'm not… I'm Catholic!" the doctor stammered.

"And what has that to do with anything? There have been many years between then and now; many travels, many marriages. And yes, many conversions. Your family extends far wider than you know." Nate remarked, then reached out to grasp the doctor's hand. "Listen Doc, the history, the mythology of what we are—some of it is true, and some is just plain crap. What we turned into when Jud killed himself are what you call vampires. *He* did this to us, and it's only by his blood that we can reverse our fates; we'll be able to live out our lives and die as we should have. Only by his blood, however diluted, can Maggie finally give birth to her child. Joshua's child." Nate's grip tightened on the quivering hand as he finished.

"*You are a sacrifice, Doc. You are going to sacrifice your life to bring another into this world.*"

With a speed not of this world, Maggie moved behind the doctor's chair, seized him by his hair and wrenched his head back. Moving it to the side, she exposed the vein pulsing so quickly; fear.

Fear meant adrenaline, adrenaline was so much like a drug to her now. She sniffed his neck, then licked the papery skin over the vein.

Nate held the older man's hand as she sank her fangs into his neck. When he felt the fingers go slack, he released it. Walking around beside Maggie, he put his arms around her. She turned, laying her cheek over his heart, listening to the faint thump-thump. As always, Nate had fed before meeting with the doctor

She gasped as the blood surged through her system, reaching the tiny fetus in her womb and bringing it to life. Within moments, her belly was stretching outwards. She could hear the tiny heartbeat inside her; looking to Nate's face, she realized he could hear it too.

She ran her hands over her new belly protectively. "Joshua. Welcome home, little one."

Nate smiled at her, his eyes glittered strangely in the deepening dark. "Now, my love. Now we will have his revenge!"

"Yes. I can feel Joshua's forgiveness already. They should have realized there would be reprisals for twisting his words." Maggie smiled gently. "But it will be some time before that can happen; at least a few years. He will grow fast as long as we keep him fed." She turned to leave the room, her rapidly expanding middle nearly getting in the way as she went through the door. She stopped, tilting her head to the side.

"Don't forget that tape, sweet. We wouldn't want to have anything hinder our progress."

Nate nodded, and turned to the bookshelf behind the couch. Reaching up, he pulled out three of the large, dusty tomes, then grabbed a fourth; inside there was a camera, still running. He chuckled.

It seemed all of Jud's family, past and recently deceased, were deceitful. Nate left the room, glancing back only once to shake his head at the doctor. Much too trusting. Much too... *devious*. Thankfully, it was done.

# Black and White

The room had been dark forever. Anna began to feel she had *never* been outside, *never* seen the light, though she knew it had only been a couple of months. Two months—almost to the day—if she could trust the scratches on the wall, and the fresh scars on her arm.

She hadn't meant to keep track of the passage of days and weeks in her flesh. Anna had begun the marks on the soft sheet-rock creating her space. She snapped out of a daze at one point, discovered she'd been digging at her arm. She lit the candle with one of the last matches, and counted fifteen bloody gouges on her forearm. There was little feeling in her flesh... delayed shock perhaps. Since then, she'd been adding a mark to her arm each time she woke from sleep.

Anna couldn't take any more chances with the integrity of the walls surrounding her. Her space was sacred, safe. Hers.

*Her* space.

Anna took shelter with a group that had decided to save themselves from any approaching zombie hordes. It had become apparent there would be no government intervention or army rescues and they'd be on their own to save themselves.

They'd encased each other inside false walls in an abandoned farmhouse, cutting small holes in the floorboards for waste. The group had drawn straws to see which unlucky soul would remain outside to finish the walls, then make a dangerous trek to remain hidden elsewhere until the threat ended.

*If only they'd truly understood, as I do.* Before the outbreak, Anna worked for the virology lab; she knew what, where and why. The vaccine they'd developed had been worse—*far worse*—than the range of diseases it had been designed to cure. *Maybe I should have told them.*

The rooms had been stocked with enough food for six weeks. She had plenty of food left; she'd begun rationing after the first thirty days thinking it unlikely that Dale would emerge any earlier than that. Throughout the first weeks she'd consumed water whenever the urge overtook her, which had been often. After counting the marks on the wall, comparing that to the number of bottles left, she'd panicked. She'd almost let the screams get away from her then, though calm quickly returned. She began rationing her water to half a bottle a day, then a quarter. Eventually it didn't matter... Anna just wasn't as thirsty as she'd once been.

Dale was supposed to stack dead and decapitated bodies throughout the house after he'd walled up the last person. Afterwards, if everything went to plan, Dale would have retired to the clock tower overlooking the town square, stocked with his own supplies of water and food, to wait out the threat.

From there he would be able to see any rescue team or survivors that came along, if any came, from any direction. And of course, he'd be safe from the zombies.

The dead bodies stacked around their hideout were meant to mislead the putrefying walkers; dead was dead to them and they left corpses alone. If they managed to keep up with *and* catch a person with a heartbeat, that person was savaged until the heart stopped beating, but immediately after they were left alone. She believed the zombies could somehow hear the heartbeats in their victims.

Before all this, she'd found out her husband had been seeing someone else. And it wasn't long after they'd begun to split their assets that Anna discovered Ramon had given her a parting gift for the end of their marriage... she carried one of the diseases her lab had created a cure for. *Thank you, Ramon.* She remembered looking down at his body after Dale had removed his head.

They all shot her a look when she began laughing. *Stupid people, easily convinced Ramon's body was eviscerated by his now-*undead *girlfriend.* When Anna noticed them watching her, she composed herself. She could wait, she had plenty of time. *Ramon is not going to get up and walk away while I'm walled up, safe and sound. I am not done with you yet, you shit,* she thought to herself. *Somehow, you will pay forever.* She shook the memories away.

The day Anna stopped hearing the horrible moaning from outside her shelter, she marked herself with a cross. From that day to this there had been twenty beeps of her watch, ten days in all. *Did I sleep through some?* She didn't think she had. Moving quietly across the tiny space, she picked up her last water bottle, carefully drawing a small sip from it.

She wondered if Dale had survived. What if he'd been killed on his way to the clock tower? What if something happened to him while he was there, or perhaps on his return?

*What if Dale was never coming back...* Anna shuddered, not bothering to stop the slip of tears from her eyes but she did bite her cheek to keep herself from sobbing out loud—blood filled her mouth but again, she felt no pain. *How long can I go without water, is it really a few days? In the end, does it really matter if Dale comes back at all?* Her thoughts raced and jumbled together, faster and faster, igniting panic she'd not felt since the early days of her self-imposed incarceration.

There was a space of two feet between each makeshift room; five rooms in all, literally filling the large family room of the old house with little cubicles. One on each wall, one in the center. One of the rooms held the couple from out of town. They'd made the mistake of vacationing during a huge nation-wide crisis, with no working phones or cell service, they had no way to get in touch with family. They'd been the first to step inside their little space. The woman had been crying. *Had she been pregnant?* Anna thought maybe she'd heard something like that, but hoped not... it was hit and miss that *they'd* survive, let alone a fetus.

She herself had been in the center space. There should have been some sound coming from either side of her—there had been in the early days, but there had been nothing for a long time.

Anna fell asleep worrying about her water and wondering how everyone else was. Wondering if they were alive.

She awoke several hours later to the beep of her watch, realizing she could hear something else. There was *someone* in the house, the footsteps determined, not sluggish. Judging from the muffled sounds, whoever it was—*Dale?*—was moving from space to space.

Anna could barely keep from yelling out, her mouth and throat trembling with her force of resistance. She dug her nails into her elbows; arms crossed and tucked over her chest to keep from even breathing too loud, an attempt to muffle her heartbeat. *Just in case.*

The footfalls went past her without stopping, and she nearly screamed for help, instead shoving the fingers of her right hand into her mouth, biting down as hard as she could. Even that didn't stop the softest whimper from escaping.

The footsteps stopped at the next space, then went around to the first again. A thudding sound began, and Anna dared to let herself hope, though she heard no voices, no sounds other than that of someone breaking into each space. She held herself still, trying not to hope too much as conflicting visions of zombie mouths rending her flesh and that of joyous rescue danced around her inner mind.

*Moaning.* It sounded so much like the unearthly, inhuman din that emanated from the zombies that she was certain they'd all been found, certain that Dale had been caught and turned and *oh god, how can I get away?* Covering her ears and leaning forward to bite down on her knee, she screamed inwardly.

Anna didn't want to die, only to walk aimlessly for eternity, or until she rotted into pieces.

It seemed as though the very air itself vibrated with a heavy thumping. Whatever it was had found her and was trying to get in, to get into *her* space. She rolled to her side, pulling herself into the fetal position. Closing her eyes as tightly as she could, Anna let herself scream. *Why not?* Whatever it was, it was going to find her anyway.

She screamed herself hoarse as the thumping and tearing continued; the wall separating her meager, slow death and that of a quick un-death crumbling apart. The light that flooded through the hole was so pure, so white and bright that it penetrated her eyelids causing an exquisite pain like none she'd ever known.

*Voices.*

Through her screams of pain and fear Anna could hear voices, feel soft hands brushing over her body and patting her back. Arms went around her as she rocked back and forth with them. She began to realize that she was not being bitten or torn asunder, there were no grasping, clawing hands. She opened her eyes.

Two young men sat across from her and a middle aged woman held her. Looking out past them, she saw the bodies of her companions lying amidst the rubble of the faux walls. Anna tried to tell them—*decapitate them!*—it might have been dehydration or starvation, but any one of them could have taken nilSTD-v5. She knew one didn't need to be bitten to become a zombie.

*Thanks to nilSTD-v5, and the human testing they'd done at the lab.*

It looked as though the young couple had decided to take their own lives—each had long gashes running down their left forearm. Even so, one never knew. Just because they were married, didn't make the sex any less dangerous. Either one could have taken nilSTD-v5 before they were married, or during, in secret.

"Who are you?" Anna asked, voice whispery-hoarse and odd-sounding, even to her own ears. Her throat was dry, but felt full of mucus. She choked a little, and the woman thumped her hard, once, on the back. A lump of solid red phlegm dislodged and Anna spit it to the ground. She stared at it, then looked around at the remains of her companions, *really seeing* them for the first time.

"We're the help, hon. It's over. That man in the clock tower, he told us how to find you all," the older woman replied. "Here dear, take my sweater… you're terribly cold."

The young men had begun packing up their equipment when they seemed to notice the change in her features; an oddly serene insanity had slipped over her face. Cold, rotting hands grasped their faces from behind, and understanding took them as they began to scream. Anna smiled.

Another of the walled-in escapees bit a chunk out of the would-be rescuer's neck. Still smiling obscenely, Anna leaned in for her own taste. As she swallowed the warm, sticky strip of muscle, she searched the stacked bodies with her eyes. *Ramon has to be here, I remember his body being tossed to one side during preparations.*

Anna rose, finding part of his body. Perhaps animals had been at it, perhaps wandering dead had ripped at it in frustration at the lack of live meat. Whatever the reason, the part that remained was the one she wanted anyway. She ripped what remained of his pants from his legs, looking with little interest at the practically hairless, wrinkled and rotting sac that contained the balls he'd shared so often with the local whores.

Anna gouged at three pieces of Ramon's body, *those parts that he had been so proud of,* tearing them right from their anchoring flesh, and tucked them into the pocket of the sweater she now wore. She would leave the nasty bits for rats to nibble on, but not here. *The lab.* She laughed hoarsely as she thought of the perfect end to Ramon's pride. *The lab. I have to remember.* She could feel the edges of her world crumbling now. *I have to get to the lab ... by all that's holy, please God, let me ... let me ... I have to ... get ... lab. Ramon—*

—her mind ground to a halt as her spirit fled the physical shell. Only her body shambled out of the house, following the others out of the door left open by their rescuers. She was hungry, and she would feed.

In the end, nothing is ever just black and white.

# It Never Lasts Forever

It was a night much like this one when I broke into the abandoned house over on Main Street—you know the one, don't you—and met Old Lady Parker. At first, I thought she was a dusty old cobweb. All I could see of her was the top of her head, so I pushed it out of the way. I knew right away something was wrong, I mean, cobwebs aren't heavy and they don't clunk when they hit a wall.

She turned around, making this horrible groaning sound. Then she kinda sighed, and *that* sounded like a knife running over sand paper. I was trying to back out of the window, barely keeping my heart in my chest. I dropped my bag, and I guess the hammer must have landed on her foot because she squealed.

I didn't stop to grab my stuff, I didn't turn around to see if she'd come out of the house either—I just scrambled out of there and beat it. My heart didn't stop racing for maybe an hour afterwards. Seriously, man, it was starting to *hurt*, it was beating so fast. Once it started to slow down though, I started getting mad. What the hell was that old woman doing down there, anyway? Think about it. The house wasn't hers, had never been hers. She didn't belong there any more than I did.

Stupid old bat. So, you know what?

Yeah... you're right. I went back. I walked straight across the yard, up the stairs, and kicked—yes, *kicked*—the door in. I was going to show her who was boss. I was going to tell her off for being there, for blowing my break-in, for scaring the shorts off me. I barged into that house raring for a fight and I didn't care if she was 80 years older than Adam, I was gonna get that fight.

You know what happened next, don't you? You figured it out yet?

Well, I'll tell you.

She wasn't on the main floor. She was still down in the basement, still under the window where I'd first come across her.

Old Lady Parker was leaning against the wall, still looking up at the window. I went up to her, grabbed her shoulder and spun her around. Man, all my tough words died in my throat, right then.

It wasn't just the feel of her skin, that was all papery and dry and kinda crackled under my fingers. It was the whole package. Her hair *was* cobwebs. There was hair under 'em but they were there. It was her *face*, man, her face was like… *gone*. I didn't think I'd pushed her that hard. And her eyes. Dude, if you think I've got creepy eyes, you shoulda seen hers. They looked like a frog's eyes. But all tiny and sunk into the sockets.

That old bat, she smiled when she saw how freaked I was. She took my hand from her shoulder, and patted it. You know, like a grandma would? Then she laughed. You ain't never heard something like that, man, or your hair would be the same color as mine.

I tried to pull my hand back, but she wouldn't let go. Kinda like I'm holding yours, now. I can see you're a bit freaked out yourself. Don't worry… I'm almost done.

I had to close my eyes, because I couldn't look at her anymore. I grabbed at her with my other hand, but it was like she wasn't there at all. I opened my mouth to scream, but nothing came out. Well, not *nothing*, it sounded like a knife on sandpaper.

When I opened my eyes, Old Lady Parker was gone.

You know it's wrong to break into houses, don't you? Well, I learned my lesson, just as you're learning yours now. This'll just take a minute, man, then I'll get out of here and you can… well, you'll just stay here. I'd like to say I'm sorry, really I would. But, I'm not.

You'll be okay. Someone will come along, eventually.

It never lasts forever.

# Ring a Ring a Rosie

The Emergency Room at Brighid's Sacred Cross Hospital in New Bedlam had experienced many nights of insanity over the years. Never as many as in recent months, where it seemed every night had its share of crazies, but probably more than any other small town ER would.

As her luck would have it, Mary Elizabeth Rose Lyn King had pulled the graveyard shift on the worst night of any month. This one was even worse, her superstitious Scottish blood told her— Friday the 13th *and* a full moon. She didn't need her old Granda to tell her to keep her guard up, but as she left the house her mind heard the voice from the parlor anyway. *Drive careful, watch for deer, take the beads and cross yourself, girl.* "Yes, Granda," she whispered. The man had been dead for years, but still she replied to a memory deep within her.

When she pulled into the staff parking area, her eyes were drawn skyward. Shining right into her car, straight through the windshield—the brightest full moon she had seen in ages. A shiver down her spine urged an involuntary crossing, after which she took the rosary from the mirror and tucked it into her pocket. *Better safe not sorry, than sin now and repent later.*

The entire place was eerily silent as she walked the slippery fifty feet to the entrance. Even the ambulance bay was quiet for once, both buses sitting cold and empty. Rose Lyn pushed through the door and into what she knew would be a hellish twelve hour shift.

*Rosie…*

The voice at the end of the hall made her hair stand on end. Not quite a scream, really not much above a whisper, Rose Lyn could have sworn her Nana Ann was calling her. Only Nana Ann called her Rosie, and only because it had been her mother's name. "Hello? Amanda, are you screwing around again, because if you are this is *so* not funny," she called down the corridor.

"Rose Lyn, I am too busy re-stocking the Lac-trays to fool around. But, I *do* have every intention of fooling around in an hour unless we get some patients in," Amanda spoke as she breezed past Rose Lyn with a dozen trays balanced in her arms. "Tony said he'd be back with dinner in half an hour. We ordered Szechuan, so if you want in and no one has cut their foot off by the time he gets here, come and join us."

Rose Lyn nodded, knowing that Tony would bring enough to feed the first floor, let alone the three of them. "I'll get my paperwork done first. Is Sherrie on tonight, or did she call in again?"

From far down the hall Amanda replied that the other woman would be in, but not until after 3 AM "If this was any other hospital, Sherrie would have been fired long ago."

She entered the staff room, hung her coat and purse in the locker, and as she was swinging the locker door shut, the voice called again—*Rosie*—only this time it was right beside her ear. A child's laughter followed and Rose Lyn felt the goosebumps rise along her arms. "Fuck!"

"What did you say, Rose Lyn?" A man's voice from the hall almost settled her nerves, but knowing it was only Tony kept her on her nerves' edge. "I thought I just heard the good Irish nun utter a curse word. I must have been mistaken, right?"

"Actually, Tony, you are quite right for once. First time for everything, isn't there?" she jibed him. "You really are on a roll these days. First Amanda, now being right. Maybe I should get you to buy me a lottery ticket!"

"You wish, baby. It'd win, and I'd take old Amanda and get the hell outta Dodge. This town sucks."

Rose Lyn laughed with the newest EMT, noting he was wearing his uniform instead of street clothes. "I didn't know you were on duty tonight. And where's dinner?"

*Rosie... Posie...*

She felt the world tilt under her feet, and she gripped the table, not hearing Tony's reply. She waved off his offer of a chair, and just shrugged when he asked if she was okay. "I think I'm starting to get Sherrie's flu."

"Uh, no you're not. Sherrie doesn't have the flu, she has a fatal attraction to Johnnie Walker."

Laughing only to soothe Tony's worry, Rose Lyn left the room and settled in at the main desk. There were still no patients in sight, other than a teenager that had come in during the previous shift and was still waiting for test results. Her perception of reality was certainly changing an hour later when she finished her paperwork and Amanda called her into the staff room for their dinner.

"I missed what you said earlier, Tony, about why you were back without this."

Tony had a mouthful so Amanda answered for him. "He'd left his wallet in the bus, so he made the order and told them he'd be back for it. What has gotten into you tonight, Rose Lyn? You're acting all weird."

"I don't know. I think I might be coming down with something." Taking a mouthful of the delicious pork and cabbage dish saved her from having to explain something she was entirely unsure of. Slipping a hand into the pocket of her scrubs, she absently rubbed the crucifix attached to her rosary. Before long, the other two were so engrossed in each other that Rose Lyn took her second helping of food out to the main desk and ate while she waited for the insanity to begin.

Three hours and a dose of Pepto later, only Sherrie had come through the doors.

"I've been working here for fifteen years, and I've never seen it so quiet on a Friday night. Never—and this one you'd think would be a doozy," Sherrie mumbled. "It's enough to send me home."

"So go home, just don't expect us to clock you out," Amanda sniped from her position on one of the exam tables. Now that the kid had been released, the entire ER was empty except for staff.

"You know, Amanda, you are a right royal bitch," Sherrie said as she stood, pushed in her chair, and stalked away from the desk. Within moments, Rose Lyn was watching the older woman's backside walk away down the hall.

When the door closed behind her and they were sure Sherrie was out of hearing distance, both she and Amanda laughed until they had tears in their eyes. "Bitch. Oh that is so rich, considering the way she treated us when we started here."

*Rosie…*

"Well, hon, I'm going to go out to the bus and have my way with Tony. You'll be alright here?" Amanda asked as she started down the hall. Without waiting for an answer or looking back, she left.

Rose Lyn hated being in the ER alone, but she knew the doc was just down the hall in the Resident's Room. It still felt as though she were the only person on the entire floor.

*Posie...*

The voice was much closer now, right behind her. When she turned to see who it was, a woman was standing there. Her gnarled hands gripped the edge of the desk and she looked as though she was about to faint. Rose Lyn jumped up, moving as quickly as she could in case the old woman were to fall.

As she slid her arms under the woman's, she nearly retched up all the wonderful dinner she'd eaten earlier. The stench radiated from the woman, as though it had permeated even her skin and hair. The clothes were torn and raggedy, looking like she'd never taken them off.

Perhaps she hadn't.

"Rosie... I've come t'see ye, girl. I have summat for ye," she spoke, her breath bringing tears to Rose Lyn's eyes and making her head swim. As she assisted the older woman onto the exam bed, she realized the smell was coming from huge red and black circles on the woman—visible on her neck and face amidst the grime and grease. When she settled the woman back against the pillows, one of the angry welts burst, and a flood of gray-black pus escaped.

Rose Lyn didn't make it to the sink to throw up.

Cleaned up and with a healthy amount of Vick's spread under her nose to counter the smell, Rose Lyn returned to continue taking history and trying to clean her up. The doctor had been paged, but so far hadn't shown his face.

She wiped the woman's face with a damp, cool cloth. Nothing seemed to lift the dirt from her skin, and she could see there were lesions there now, as well. As gently as she could, Rose Lyn woke the woman to ask her what had happened.

"I've come from away t'give ye a gift, Rosie. Give summat back t'was given by yer line." The woman struggled to sit up, seeming to grow dirtier and more... *decomposed*... with each move. "Come ye closer, girl. I want t'whisper in yer ear."

Rose Lyn couldn't help herself; as much as she struggled, something compelled her to lean forward and let the old lady have her wish. As she did so, the woman grabbed her chin in claws strong as vise grips. Rose Lyn struggled in vain.

"Yer kin brought t'death wi'em, and now I gives it back."

A stream of thick, bloody vomit erupted from between the woman's lips, splattering directly onto Rose Lyn's face. Immediately, it was as though the area around the bed had been surrounded by children, laughing and chanting; Rose Lyn stumbled backwards and again heaved her own stomach contents down over her scrubs and onto the floor.

Screaming over the cacophony created by the children, she turned to the sink, desperate to get the woman's vileness from her own face. Panic and nausea set in as she realized it was in her mouth, and that started off another round of retching and vomiting.

*Ring a ring a Rosie…*

*A pocket full of posies…*

The last thing Rose Lyn saw before she crumpled to the floor were the laughing, smiling faces of seven filthy, rag-wearing children surrounding the woman she had tried to help.

She was in a tunnel of some sort, but not just any tunnel; it seemed to be a maze connecting many hovels together. A community? Underground? She could see doorways in the faded light cast by the torches, could hear voices echoing around her.

Rose Lyn clutched at the dirty shift she now wore, shivering in the damp cold. Somewhere off to her left, a woman cried out in grief, followed by a man's voice hushing the woman, consoling her. As much as she wanted to follow those sounds, she turned to the right, toward the sounds of glass clinking and laughter.

One hand on the slime-covered wall behind her, the other still clutching the shift that had replaced her scrubs, she inched along. Rough voices with heavy Scots accents reached her from behind a well lit door. The men were drunk, that was obvious even through their brogue. As she stumbled into the room, the woman behind the bar came at her, scolding her.

"*Muirne Ròs*, what d'ye think yer about? Get ye back to yer bed a'fore ye be passin' that blight to t'rest of us." She held the rag she'd been wiping the bar with over her mouth, and stood back from Rose Lyn. "Get ye gone, girl."

"Where am I? How did I get here?" Rose Lyn asked, trying to tumble the words over a tongue unused to speaking English. She was startled to hear her own voice, but with the heavy brogue the others used.

"Aye, yer fever has taken yer head now, girl. Get ye gone, get ye back to yer bed!"

Rose Lyn took another step toward the woman, holding out one hand as she did so. She saw her hand was covered in the same putrescent black flesh as the old woman in the ER. She stopped still, dropping the material of her shift to stare at both her of arms and the blackness covering them. "*NO!* What is this? What is this?" she scratched at the skin, trying to peel it back as though it were nothing more than Hollywood latex. As her grimy nails broke the skin, pus flowed more than blood.

Looking up, she was stunned to see that the woman had backed off farther yet, and the men—so jovial in their drunken state only moments before—had abandoned their stools and were now pressed against the far wall.

"Lochlan, run down to MacDonnough's and fetch back the doc. The fever's taken the lass."

Rose Lyn backed up until she was pressed against a wall, herself. "No, no, no, no, no... I don't understand, I don't... I want to go home!"

*Rosie...*

Rose Lyn screamed as she woke, strapped to an exam table with the soft restraints generally reserved for the suicidal. She glanced around, seeing her co-workers on either side of the bed, but unable to find the old woman who attacked her.

"What... what happened? Where is the old woman?"

"Rose Lyn, honey, there was no one here except you. Doc heard you scream and when he got here, he found you on the floor."

"But, there was an old woman in here, a street person. She was sick, and I was trying to help her, but then she grabbed me and threw up all over. She had kids with her."

"There was no one but you in here, Rose Lyn." Tony spoke quietly. "I mean, come on—the place has been dead all night. And besides, if someone had come in, Amanda and I would have seen them. We were right outside."

"She didn't come from the front, she came up from behind the desk." Now, thinking back, Rose Lyn realized that would have been nearly impossible. "I know that sounds crazy, but it's true. I even had to change and put Vick's under my nose. She smelled so bad."

Doctor Fields was checking her pulse when he told her she didn't have Vick's under her nose, and she was wearing the same scrubs now as when she had arrived. Rose Lyn saw his eyebrow twitch as he made note of the jump in her heartbeat when his words sank in. "She was here, I know she was."

"Rose Lyn, I believe you're coming down with something. You've got a mild fever, and it may have spiked. That's all, a fever induced hallucination."

"No, *NO!* She was here. And so were those children."

"Rose, sweetie, why don't you just rest out what's left of your shift. Tony and I will get you home later, ok?" Amanda used her nurse-voice on Rose Lyn; it was then she realized there was no arguing with them... if she did, she could end up taking a trip to the third floor west wing in a wrap-around jacket.

Coming to her decision, she nodded and putting her head down on the pillow, closed her eyes. As soon as she did, vertigo took over and made her feel even worse. Her friends' voices drifted farther away until they were nothing but an annoying drone in the background.

*Rosie...*

When she opened her eyes again, it was time to go home.

*Ring a ring a Rosie...*
*Pocket full of posies...*

Rose Lyn sat up in bed, her hands wrapped tight in the sheets, her body drenched in a cold sweat. For what must have been the fortieth time in two weeks, she'd dreamed of those children and that horrible chant they'd been singing when she'd been attacked. She waited until her heart stopped pounding before swinging her feet from the bed and making her way across the room in the dark. Not even a scrap of moonlight came through the open window; hearing a distant rumble of thunder, Rose Lyn pulled the window down and latched it.

From her experience, nothing would allow her to return to sleep after that dream, that *nightmare*. Every nap, every night's sleep, interrupted with those voices and that chant.

As a child, Rose Lyn had loved Ring Around a Rosie. Her grandmother used to play it with her, telling her it was a rhyme all the way from the times of war and strife in England, the Wars of the Roses. Supposedly it was how at the end of the wars, the two families became one; Lancaster married York and the red rose and the white rose became the bi-colored Tudor Rose. In the end, the house of Tudor fell to the Stuarts.

A five year old didn't find anything interesting in the games of war, but dancing the ring was always fun. It wasn't until she was much older that she learned the other stories behind the rhyme. Small pox, the plague—the connections all no more than old wives' tales.

Rose Lyn stopped reminiscing, closing the curtains as she stepped back from the window. Deciding a mug of tea would remedy the doldrums, she headed toward the kitchen to put the kettle on. As she passed her grandparent's old room, now her library, she caught sight of movement, as though someone were in the room. "Hello?"

*Rosie… come play with us, Rosie…*

"Who's there? Get out of my house, whoever you are!" Steeling her nerves, she pushed the door open further and was immediately assailed by the rancid stench of unwashed, disease-ridden bodies. Before she'd taken even two steps into the room, tiny, dirty hands pulled on her nightgown, dragging her to the center of the room. The children surrounded her, beginning the dance.

*Ring a ring a Rosie…*
*A pocketful of posies…*
*Ashes to ashes…*

Rose Lyn broke free of their circle, running out to the hall and down the stairs. Without stopping to grab her keys, she left the house. Irrationally, she tried to escape in the car only to realize much too late that the keys were still hanging at the door.

Leaving the car door open, she walked up the path toward the house, hoping the children were gone. Nothing but a nightmare, she'd never really woken up from it. Perhaps she was still asleep on her bed, fighting the nasty scene from there.

Halfway to the steps, the children surrounded her again; Rose Lyn fell to her knees, screaming.

As her eyes adjusted to the dark, she saw a giant bird standing next to her bed. Rose Lyn could hear its ragged breathing, and as it shuffled closer she saw it had hands, *human* hands, sticking out from a creaky covering. The smell of damp leather enveloped her. The bird was featherless, but *wearing* leather...

"Muirne Ròs, do you know where you are?" it asked, the words muffled as they slipped from the stiff beak. "You're in your home, Muirne. You're ill. Seems your mother brought something back from the docks down here to the Close. I'm afraid she has not survived, but I believe I just may save you."

"Who...?" Rose Lyn cringed away from the leather-bound bird, shrinking against the cold wall behind her. "I'm not..."

"Shush, girl. I am Doctor Rae. I've drained the disease from your flesh, and kept you here under guard. Do you feel as though you could drink some broth?"

"What do you mean, disease? I'm not *Murren Rose*, I'm *Rose Lyn*! Where...what is this place?"

"Perhaps your fever hasn't broken after all. Sit still, or I'll have the guard hold you down." The bird pushed Rose Lyn down hard against the bed, pulled back the dirty sheet covering her and lifted the shift below; uncaring of her state of dress and mind, he poked and prodded rather roughly. When he pushed his fingers into a spot just below her right armpit, she squealed in pain.

"Ah, more buboes. That would explain your delirium. They will need to be drained so you must lie still." Doctor Rae disappeared into the darkness of the room, where Rose Lyn could hear him shuffling his feet, digging through something, metal clanking... Fear was welling up into her throat and although she wished to cry, it seemed her body had nothing left to tear with.

She ran her hands over herself, not recognizing anything of this form. Small, firm breasts, a stomach so flat it was almost concave, pelvic bones jutting against the skin. She'd never been this skinny, even as a young child. This form was nothing short of a flesh covered rack of bones.

The doctor returned with a lit candle in one hand, and an object that caught the candlelight in the other. The flash almost blinded Rose Lyn—she squeezed her eyes shut tight, knowing it was a knife.

The handle was bone, the blade was covered in a rust colored stain... *blood!*

Rose Lyn squirmed away from the approaching bird-man-doctor, trying to scramble over the back of the bed to effect an escape, she didn't want that dirty thing touching her. She screamed as she realized there just wasn't anywhere to go.

The man who stood guard outside the door entered as Rose Lyn's first scream rent the air. He too, was covered in leather, but wore no bird mask over his face. Rose Lyn could see his face showed the signs of wear only a great illness would bring. Despite that he picked her up effortlessly, depositing her on the bed once more. "D'ye want me t'old 'er down, Rae?"

"Yes, Angus, please. Give her that bit of leather to bite on, would you? It wouldn't do for the others to hear more of her screaming when they are trying to rest."

"Aye, an' th'Close is naught b'echoes in dark o'night." Angus pulled a leather strap from his pocket and pushed it into Rose Lyn's mouth, grabbing her wrist before she could pull it out. Holding her arms down firmly, he leaned over her and smiled. "Ye'll be wantin' tha' wee bit when th'doc starts in to cuttin'."

Rose Lyn cried as the scalpel tore into the flesh under her arm. She felt the hot, sticky pus run down her side, smelled the rot of it. Bile rose in her throat, thick with the perfume of death, choking...

*Rosie... Posie...*

*Come play with us, Rosie...*

The sound of children singing a nursery rhyme over and over again woke her. Rose Lyn opened her eyes slowly, the grit of sleep digging and scratching at her tear ducts. She tried to wipe at them, but found her wrists bound in soft, fleece-lined restraints. Blinking rapidly to clear her eyes, she raised her head and looked around. The room was familiar only in that all the rooms in the Brighid's Sacred Cross Hospital were decorated in an identical manner. At least she knew where she was, but she didn't understand why she was restrained, or why she was in hospital to begin with.

What floor she was on depended entirely on which nurse came to attend her. The restraints gave her enough freedom to feel around the edge of the bed, where she found the call button; relieved, she squeezed it tight between her fingers and used her thumb to press the button. *If only they'd stop singing!*

A young nurse entered the room several minutes later, one Rose Lyn did not recognize. As she tried to speak, her throat closed on itself and she began to cough. The nurse offered a drink of water, holding the glass as Rose Lyn sipped through a straw. "Is that better?"

"Yes, I think so. Thank you." Rose Lyn's throat and vocal chords were extremely sore, as though she'd suffered strep throat or tonsillitis. "Why am I here?"

"I can't tell you that, I've only just come on duty. Doctor Fields has rounds in about a half hour, if you can wait that long, or I can call the night nurse in."

"Please. Is… which floor am I on?" Rose Lyn held her breath, closing her eyes tight; the nightmare of the last while led her to believe she'd be on the third floor, the psychiatric ward. Rose Lyn could hardly hear herself over the sound of the children.

*Ring a ring a Rosie…*

"You're in the general ward, Rose Lyn. Where else would you be?" The young nurse laughed softly as she left the room, calling back over her shoulder: "Nurse Ames will be right in, I'm sure."

*Nurse Ames.* The older woman had been on staff here forever, Rose Lyn had been terrified of her as a child. Even now, working as an equal, she occasionally entertained thoughts of Ames carrying a syringe full of Pentothal to inject unsuspecting staff and patients with.

*A pocket full of Posies…*

Fields entered the room on his rounds before Ames showed up. "Rose Lyn, how are you feeling this morning? Do you remember anything?"

She shook her head. "I don't know why I'm here, Fields. Have I been sick? Did I get whatever that woman had?"

Fields sighed deeply, and made notes in Rose Lyn's chart. "There was no woman, Rose Lyn. We've been through that. You're here because your neighbor called 911; you were on your front lawn, in nothing but your pajamas, passed out. When he tried to help you into your house, you attacked him, screaming about birds and knives. He slapped you, you went out like a light, and here you are."

Rose Lyn didn't reply. She simply motioned with her hands, silently requesting that he remove the restraints. When he shook his head, apologizing softly, she closed her eyes again.

"I truly am sorry, Rose Lyn. Until we can be sure you won't do something stupid, you'll just have to remain in those… I know it's uncomfortable, and I know you'd rather just go home.

"I have to tell you, Rose. You've been placed on sick leave from work, and we've recommended that you be examined by Adamson."

"Why? Because I've been sick? You're calling in the psychiatrist because I've been sick?"

"No, Rose Lyn. I'm calling him in because you were rambling about being infected with the plague. You were hysterical, you were violent, and you had no idea who you were. You kept screaming that you weren't someone named *Murren Rose*." Fields took her fingers in his hand. Once, they'd been just a little more than friends. The show of affection touched her, and she stopped struggling, opening her eyes again.

"James... What's wrong with me?"

"That's what we're going to find out, Rose. We won't let you down."

With a final squeeze, he turned and left the room. Rose Lyn stared at the ceiling, counting the dots on each tile until Ames finally appeared with a small bowl, a wash cloth and a fresh johnnie.

*Ashes to ashes...*

"Well, if it isn't little Rose Lyn. I see you aren't doing so wonderfully, now." Ames seemed to have a smirk in her voice, to go with the smirk on her face. "How's it feel to be a patient here again, after working here?"

"Just fucking wonderful. I don't want a bath."

"Language! What would your sainted grandmother say if she knew you spoke to me that way?"

"I'm sure the two of you would cluck over tea about the fate of the world..." Rose Lyn chewed her lip for a moment, knowing antagonizing Ames wasn't going to help her. "I'm sorry, Ames. I just..."

"Now, now. No need, child. I know how frustrating it is to wake up in a hospital bed. Never the less, watch the language, would you?" Ames smiled as she began washing Rose Lyn's face and arms. "You've had a hard few days, and I doubt, from the smell of you, that you've showered." The smile faltered as the nurse found the smell wasn't washing away.

"What in God's name have you been into, Rose Lyn? You stink of death."

Rose Lyn shrugged. She couldn't smell anything different. She was starting to think the old woman in the ER had somehow burned her filth into her nose. "I have no idea, Ames. I have no idea."

When Ames lengthened the straps on the restraints in order to wash Rose Lyn's body down and change her johnnie, they caught a nose full of the scent and it turned their stomachs sour. Dark, bloody pus created huge stains on the johnnie and bits of skin stayed behind as it was finally pried from Rose Lyn.

"Oh my God, Rose Lyn!" Ames pulled her hands back, covering her mouth as she caught sight of Rose Lyn's sides and chest. Black pockets leaked fluids all over the bed, the pus and blood were varying in shades. "Oh, you poor thing!"

Craning her neck, Rose Lyn saw what Ames was seeing—what she herself had seen in her nightmares. Buboes. *Plague.*

The world swam and dove around her, swirling to the music of Ames' screaming, the door slamming shut, an alarm going off somewhere. Rose Lyn laid back against the pillows and began to laugh.

*Ring a ring a Rosie…*
*A pocketful of posies…*
*Ashes to ashes…*

The children came for her again, smoothing her hair from her forehead, smiling down at her, releasing her from the restraints and pulling dirty clothes around her. Rose Lyn glanced toward the door; one small boy held it shut while Fields, Ames and Adamson pounded on the outside.

Rose Lyn smiled at the children, holding her hands to them. Dancing in the circle, she joined in their song.

*Ring a ring a Rosie…*
*A pocketful of posies…*
*Ashes to ashes…*
*We all fall dead.*

# The Lion Roared

The clunking noise from behind the firewall of the beat-up '74 Malibu had become progressively louder for over an hour. No matter how many times Emmy turned the stereo up, it didn't seem to take too long before the sound over-powered the heavy bass beat.

There was a moment when she thought she could feel the noise right through the gas pedal; Emmy could have sworn the pedal pushed back at her foot. Telling herself it was just nerves from driving through the storm, she kept on, eyes straining in their sockets as though the simple act of bulging out a bit would give them super powers.

That was what she really needed—super powers. Infra-red vision to see through the swirling snow or laser eyes to burn through the harder drifts. *Screw that*, Emmy thought, *I'd super power up a bubble and just float there*. Swearing under her breath, she admitted she wasn't even entirely sure where *there* was… Brad's map had been of little help for a city chick.

Emmy tore her focus from the road for just one second to flick her lighter and touch the flame to the tip of the cigarette that had dangled from her lips for a half hour. In that one moment, some kind of dog wandered out onto the road; she saw the red reflection of the animal's eyes barely in time, and she swerved while hitting the brakes.

She didn't hit the dog, but there was one final, catastrophic *BANG* from the motor of the Malibu. After trying several times to restart the vehicle, Emmy gave up, swearing profusely as she spent several minutes digging through her purse, looking for her cell phone. The profanities increased in volume and intensity when she realized the phone wasn't even in her purse. Leaning back with eyes closed, Emmy tried to calm herself.

Leaving the city had been a bad idea. Brad had insisted she make the five hour trip to his family's vacation home to meet the parents. Emmy hadn't realized that driving in the middle of a storm was a bad idea; she drove in all weather in the city and had never had a problem. And at least in the city, if she had an accident, she'd only have to walk a few feet to find help.

She glanced out the window, hoping to see some form of life, despite knowing there hadn't been any lights along this road for some time. If there was a dog out wandering the roads, there had to be some sort of civilization close. *Even a farmer would be a happy sight right now.* Emmy turned the lights and ignition off, her watch catching her eye as she did so. The luminous dial showed her she was now an hour late for the dinner…perhaps Brad and his family would come looking for her.

Switching the ignition back to 'Accessory,' Emmy switched CDs and settled in for a bit of a wait.

She woke with a start. Cursing herself for falling asleep, she tried to figure out where the beeping noise was coming from. Emmy could barely move her fingers she was so cold, but rummaged through the trash on the floor until she found the source of the annoying beep.

Her cell phone; only now did she recall plugging it into the outlet on the dash. She pushed the talk button, to be met with whistling static and white noise.

"Hello?" she yelled. "Hello? Anyone there…I need help!"

"Emmy?" Brad's voice broke through the static and her heartbeat quickened. "Emmy, where are you? You're late, and we've waited dinner on you!"

"Brad, I think I'm lost and I nearly had an accident; I can't get the car to start again. Can't you come and get me?"

Static had overtaken the phone again, but she thought she could make out Brad's voice behind it. It sounded as though he was talking to someone else.

"Did you stick to the map, Emmy?" he asked.

"No Brad, I decided to go exploring in the hills in an area I've never been to before, right in the middle of a damn blizzard! What the hell do you think?"

"All right, all right, I'm sorry. What happened?"

Emmy pulled the phone from her ear and looked it. *How could he be so stupid? Didn't I just tell him?* "I nearly hit a dog, and after the

53

car stopped, so did the motor. I've tried to get it started, but it won't. I'm getting really cold, Brad."

"Yeah, when it storms on the first of March, it's always really cold. There should be an emergency kit in the glove-box though, open it up and light some candles. And there's a blanket in the back. Can you tell me what the dog looked like?"

Frustrated, Emmy bit back a smart-assed response. First of all, she knew it could be cold in March. Generally, the weather was the same in the city as it was here; only the snow didn't swirl around as intensely.

"Emmy? You there?" Brad's voice again.

"Yeah, sorry. Look, there was a lot of snow, all I could see was shaggy fur, pointy ears and red eyes. That could describe pretty much any dog ever born."

"Nah, there's only a few that'll have red eyes when light hits them. They gotta have blue eyes for them to glow red. Only blue eyed dogs around here are the Wilson huskies...you're about fifteen minutes away, it won't take us long to come and rescue you. Ok?"

"Yeah...you might want to bring a tow rope though. Are you sure about that eye thing?"

"Yes, Emmy, I am. We'll have to leave the car there until the storm passes. After that, Dad and I will take the tractor out and get it out."

*Tractor?* Emmy thought. *Why on earth would they need a tractor at what is supposed to be a vacation home?* "All right, just hurry." She pushed the end button before he could respond.

This was going to be the last weekend with him. He'd been getting on her nerves for some time, but his nonchalance and flippancy on the phone just now sealed it. Emmy had a tickle at the back of her neck that usually signified trouble...she'd passed it off as the storm and her situation. Now she thought it was signaling the end of her relationship.

She searched the glove-box for the kit Brad had mentioned, but couldn't find it. There wasn't a blanket in the back either, so Emmy wrapped her arms around herself and tucked her chin to her chest. *If they don't get here soon*, she thought, *all they'll find is a frozen corpse.*

Emmy wasn't sure how much time had passed. She had fallen asleep again, and now the battery had worn down—it was not only dark but silent as well. Looking outside of the car, she saw that the storm had lessened quite a bit; she could see a light only a few yards from where she sat shivering. Without over-thinking it, she grabbed her purse and cell phone, and left the car. Since it was Brad's crappy vehicle, she left the keys in it. If someone came along and wanted to steal it, she no longer cared.

Outside the snow was deep but loose, so it wasn't too hard to walk through. The stars were beginning to peek through the remainders of the cloud cover, and the wind had stilled entirely. The silence, as declared so often, was deafening.

Emmy found the driveway to the nearest house by noting the difference in the way the snow was piling up on it. There was only the one outdoor light for the entire house, and as she drew nearer, she saw it ran on a large battery attached to it—an emergency light like those at the college she and Brad attended.

Knocking on the door, Emmy prayed someone was home. She stood shivering and puffing clouds of vapor from her mouth. She knocked again, and waited—still there was no answer. Finally, Emmy decided to try the door herself, and found it unlocked. Blessing her luck, she walked into her new shelter.

There were faces pressed to the window, staring at her.

Emmy could feel their eyes on her, even as she roused herself from a dreamless sleep.

There were three; they couldn't have been any more than ten years old, any of them. They had their hands cupped around their eyes, noses pressed firmly against the frigid glass. Emmy couldn't place what bothered her most—that they just stood there staring at her, or that they were completely silent, motionless. She stretched her legs as she pulled herself into a sitting position on the dusty old couch. She waved to the children at the window.

They didn't wave back, they didn't move. Frustrated, tired and hungry, Emmy didn't feel like dealing with the local smart-ass children; she flipped her middle finger at them on her way past the window.

She rustled through the nearly empty cupboards, discovering tins of food she didn't or couldn't recognize; the wrappers had been torn off most of them. After a pretty thorough search of the drawers, she finally found something that could be used to open a can. She could at least eat something, even if it was condensed soup, without water or heat. What she found in the first can made her retch.

*A piece of finger.*

Her appetite completely doused, she took another look at the crap in the can she'd opened. She looked closely, then poked the pink bits floating in a sea of red sauce, and realization dawned. The can was full of cocktail weenies. She laughed.

Emmy ate them with her fingers, even though she was no longer hungry. She walked through to the living room again, and was startled to see that the children still stood at the window. She grabbed her purse with sauce-stained fingers, carrying it into the kitchen where she sat at the table and tried to raise a signal on her phone.

Absolutely no bars showed in either of the battery power or the signal symbols. *Great,* she thought to herself, *he gets me out here in the middle of nowhere, with no service, no people except those pod children at the window, and I have no way to find him.*

A few, silent tears escaped her tightly shut eyes. *Fifteen minutes to get to me, yeah right. We are so over, Brad.*

It was getting dark again. Emmy had chanced another look into the living room; the pod children were still pressed to the window. She was exhausted, but there was no way she was going to try and sleep on that couch, with those things watching her. No way in hell.

She'd made the rounds of the cabin—and it was a cabin, not a real house as far as she was concerned—checking the other rooms; mostly she was doing this so she wouldn't want find herself suddenly confronted by some insane country bumpkin with a gun. After securing the locks on the only door, she moved upstairs, into one of the tiny bedrooms. Emmy had discovered that the beds both smelled of mold and rot, but the one in her chosen room was a lot better than the others.

She closed the door tight, pushed a chair under the doorknob, and stretched out on the bed. She didn't cover up, in fact she didn't open the bed up at all, only lay down on the covers. *I used my jacket as a blanket last night, I can do the same tonight.*

It wasn't long before Emmy's eyes began to close and she sighed, slipping into a half-sleep state.

*Somewhere in the dark Emmy could hear thumping, clanking and banging, occasionally interspersed with colorful language she herself was known to use. She knew she'd locked the door, and was sure the noise she was hearing was all in her imagination.*

*The laughter of several children floated up to her from somewhere beneath her. Emmy's eyes snapped open; she was now fully awake. A male and female voice joined those of the children, Emmy thought she recognized them. She was almost certain she'd talked to that voice, the woman's voice, on the phone before. Emmy was almost positive the woman was Brad's sister.*

*She rose slowly, almost silently slipping to the door and pulling it open. Emmy cringed when the hinges protested with what really sounded like a young girl screaming. She quietly made her way down the stairs and at the door to the kitchen she stopped, and tried to call out; her throat closed and she felt as though she would be sick. Hysteria caused her body to shake uncontrollably. The children from the window smiled at her from their places at the little table, the woman stood near the old fashioned cook-stove, and the man was building the fire inside it.*

*When they turned around, Emmy saw they were missing their faces.*

She woke to her own screams pealing into the silence of the bedroom. Light was seeping in through the window now, and she knew she'd actually slept, and deeply. Her stomach rumbled and she felt a pressing need to relieve herself. She swung her legs over the edge of the bed, putting her feet on the floor. It seemed a *lot* warmer in the room now than it had when she'd first come in.

The hair on her arms rose as she reached the door…the chair was back in its place against the wall, and the door was open a crack. *How did that happen? How* could *it happen?* Emmy opened it the rest of the way, listening carefully before she stepped out into the hallway. The dream rose to her mind as she heard a noise coming from the kitchen. Her breath started to hitch in her chest; she had to bite her lip hard, drawing blood, to keep herself from screaming.

Scared as she'd never been before, Emmy never the less stepped out into the hall, peering through the dim light. Her eyes felt like they would pop out of her skull, and her skin felt as though it were burning and freezing in turns. She made her way down the stairs, feeling a sense of déjà vu like never before.

Brad stood beside the cook-stove. Someone, she assumed his father, was stoking the fire in it. When Brad saw Emmy standing there, he smiled and started towards her, but she backed up a step.

She'd moved far enough that she could look through into the living room, and there were the children, pressed against the glass, just as they'd been the day before. It seemed to Emmy that they'd switched positions. She avoided Brad's reaching arms and with a deep breath, walked to the window. Moving from one to the other, she stared directly into the eyes of each child.

They weren't...*right*. They weren't real, but they also weren't *right*. And she was positive they were in different positions.

"I see you've met the Martin triplets," Brad spoke. At Emmy's confused glance, he continued. "When old man Martin's wife went crazy, she locked the boys out in the cold during a storm. When Martin managed to get home, he found them like this...pressed against the glass, looking in. Somehow, they'd died like that—all three of them," Brad spoke. "He found his wife in the kitchen, with her face practically melted onto the cook-stove. She'd literally fried herself on the top."

Emmy couldn't stop looking at the children. She heard what Brad was saying, though it wasn't sinking in. Something was not right with those children. And their mother...she'd sounded so much like Brad's sister!

Brad's father came into the room, introducing himself as Michael; he carried on with the story. "Martin had those little statues built of the boys not long after the funerals. Each one has a piece of the dead child inside it. He never told anyone which piece, and the guy that made them—he died before he even finished. They're not completely painted, but you can only tell during the summer. Martin put them there, against the glass. If you ask me, he was loonier than his wife."

Emmy turned to them, finally breaking eye contact with the one she felt was the leader, the oldest. "They've moved."

Brad and his father exchanged a look, one Emmy was not blind to. They knew something.

"What? What is it?" she asked.

"Old man Martin, he used to come into town once in a while and tell people the boys had been in the house at night. He came in less and less over the years, but when he stopped all together, some folks in town drove out to check on him. He'd been dead a while, you understand. About a week I'd guess, from the rumors.

"He died the same way his wife did, face first onto the cook-stove. Thing is, his nose, cheekbones and jaw had been smashed.

There were bruises on the back of his neck and on his arms, funny shaped bruises. Little hands," Brad replied.

Emmy turned to the boys again. The looked like innocent little lambs, peeking into an abandoned house. She was sure they were grinning at her.

"March it was." Brad's father was now lost in memory. "The first of March that year was deadly cold, and the storm blew up outta nowhere. One moment it was clear and sunny, colder than a penguin's ass, next thing it was so thick no one could see the ends of their own noses. The lion roared that year."

Brad nodded. "The month went out like a lamb though, innocent as could be. Just like the boys there. Innocent."

As Emmy watched, one of the smiles grew wider, one frost-covered eyelid winked down.

The lion had roared again…and the *innocent* had things to do.

# The Legless Ones

A long time ago, this island was inhabited not only by the Fae and the men, but also by every creature ever imagined. And you know, maybe there were some that most mortals *didn't* imagine, too.

Not everyone could see those creatures, of course. The Fae could see everything, and the half-Fae could see most things. Only the very gifted of the men could see past their livestock. If they'd been able to see the wings on the cows and the horse-like tails on the chickens, how would they have reacted?

But ... they could not see. That's how we get to the story of The Legless Ones, three beings that once had legs. Before they raised the ire of the Good Father, that is. Their mother, D'ana, really should have kept a better rein on them. The Good Father kept her so busy, though, she had to leave the newborns in the care of their siblings.

The boys were born on a cold evening in the midst of the lambing season. A fog had rolled in from the hills, and the meadows were peaceful but for the occasional bleating from the livestock. D'ana and her consort, Allathair, had been busy visiting all the farms of men, blessing the ewes and lambs as they dropped. It was in the midst of this that D'ana felt a tug at her womb, and one, two, three, there they were. Allathair patted each on the head, told them to behave and, as all divine beings seem to do, moved on with his work. D'ana took the boys to the mounds under the mountains, where she and Allathair had made their home.

The other children glared at the newcomers. A sound like running water rose in the room as the twin sisters, Boann and Sinann, cried out in protest. They were the oldest and would be stuck caring for the three ugly boys their mother had brought home. A brilliant light dazzled the eyes as Lugh and Luna added their complaints.

D'ana raised her hand; the room darkened and fell quiet. She told the older children they must care for the new siblings, but that the three boys would have to go out and make their own way in the coming months, just as their older brother and sisters had done. She showed her children how the boys had grown, even in the few minutes since they'd entered the mound.

Grudgingly, the siblings agreed to watch over the triplets, though they were rather ugly. Boann and Sinann secretly blamed the rolling fog for the triplets' conception, claiming some man had cloaked himself in it and managed to bed their mother whilst Allathair slept. Lugh laughed, sending showers of golden light from his head as he did so. He pointed out that the boys had four legs and tails—they couldn't be of the men, who had just two legs and no tails.

Luna smiled at her new brothers, thinking to herself that they resembled the dragons who danced the fields in fall, after the harvests. Of course, the others would never have seen them. Sinann and Boann didn't like walking the fields, and Lugh never went out at night. Still, she didn't want to get stuck making sure the three stayed out of trouble. As her mother turned to leave the mound, she hid herself in the voluminous robes and made her escape.

She managed to get to the horizon before her mother noticed her and scolded her. Showing only half her face, Luna remained rebellious and rode the skies for the rest of the night.

Meanwhile, the three older siblings faced the three youngest on either side of the dinner table. The triplets opened their mouths, and a horrible screeching echoed through the mounds, rather than the language all deities are born knowing. Sinann recoiled when she saw their tongues were thin and forked. She rolled her eyes as she left, Boann following quickly behind, but not before silencing the triplets with a douse of icy water.

After the sisters had gone, the triplets started up with their cacophony once more. Lugh covered his ears, yelling at them to shut their mouths. He guessed it was only fair, his sisters had taken care of him when he first arrived, and now it was his turn to take care of the younger siblings. He didn't have anything else to do anyway—at least for several hours. He watched, mildly amused, as the three identical boys began eating items off the floor.

What could he do to keep them occupied while he slept?

An idea came to him then.

"You three, come here. Tell you what… you're hungry, but I'm no good at gathering food. There are farms around here with lots of interesting things to eat, so why don't you go out and find those? Don't forget how to get back here, and don't come back until you've each eaten three chickens, three piglets, and three lambs."

Lugh covered his ears again as the boys discussed their options. They really couldn't eat Lugh—and were glad he couldn't understand what they were saying, as he was still bigger than they were—and they *were* hungry.

Two turned to the door, while the third turned to Lugh, nodding, then followed his brothers outside. Off they went, the sound of Lugh's laughter following them.

The three roved the countryside, pillaging whenever they came across a yard with livestock. Not long before the dawn crept over the edges of the mountains, the triplets returned to the mound to find Lugh snoring.

He awoke, startled not only by the noise of his brothers' return, but also by their condition as they stood over him. Each one was covered over in animal blood, and one had the partially gnawed remains of a chicken stuck in his hair. Lugh's eyes passed over the boys in turn, realizing they were now just as tall and broad as he.

"Clean yourselves before Mother and Father see you," he said, and left them to it. He had business of his own to attend.

In a flash, Lugh was gone, immediately replaced by his sister, Luna. She groaned in frustration when she saw the state the boys were in, but helped them get cleaned up anyway. Sinann and Boann entered the mound only moments before their parents, leaving a trail of icy water on the floor. None of them knew what the boys had been up to—the triplets were as clean and strange looking as when they were born, only much bigger.

*They were now fully grown.*

D'ana took them in her arms for a hug, then settled them in for a nap before she took them out to meet their neighbors. These, of course, were the lesser gods; the boys would have to learn to accept their homage.

Thus passed the first day of their lives.

Early in the evening, Allathair and D'ana left the mound to tend to their blessings. Sinann and Boann followed not long after, swearing Luna and Lugh to secrecy without giving their youngest brothers a second glance.

It wasn't long before Luna melted away, and Lugh was once more left with the four-legged siblings.

"You three did so well last night, why don't you go out and find yourselves some more fun tonight? You might want to go farther out, though. You sure did cause a stir among the men!"

All three nodded their assent, and removed themselves from Lugh's presence. They didn't like him anyway; the room was always too hot when he was home.

Many months passed, and one warm summers eve, D'ana was confronted by Allathair while they blessed the fields.

"The men are beseeching us to find out what is killing the livestock, my love. I think we both know what has happened. Don't deny it, you have had the same suspicions. The youngest of our brood have created a serious problem, and we must act."

"Allathair, I can not believe any child of ours would cause such destruction and dissent. Please, can we not look elsewhere first?" D'ana wrung her hands as she spoke to her husband. Not only did she have the same suspicions, she'd actually caught the boys during one of the raids. What they'd done to the cattle had been frightening, even to her.

"No love, act we must, and now it must be." He took her hand and led her behind a large mound. He comforted her briefly before turning her head so she could see the havoc taking place in the pasture beyond.

When D'ana nodded, Allathair moved past the mound and called out to his sons. The only response they gave him were three identical sneers as their teeth tore into an old plow-horse. The animal screamed in pain, and Allathair was forced to act. He quickly stepped closer and held out his hand, muttering in the old tongue.

The horse stilled, but his children whined and hissed in protest.

"You have broken the laws of our people, all three of you. We've tried to teach you to eat what is given you by our subjects, but you've taken from them the very gifts that sustain us. You will be punished!" Allathair's voice boomed out over the fields, causing Luna to cower behind thickening clouds, and Lugh to slip closer to his family. Boann and Sinann came to stand by their mother where they could snicker at the trouble the boys had found themselves in.

"You—old man. Mussssn't interfere. Can not. We needssss the Mother. Sssshee lovessss usssss," three voices responded to

Allathair's words. All the boys moved as one, as though to strike their Father down where he stood.

D'ana stepped out. When they saw her coming towards them, they slunk backward, hissing to themselves. The cadence to their unapologetic voices broke her last hope of salvaging her family.

"I stand with your Father. You have done wrong. Face your punishment properly, as befitting your status!"

"No!" the boys cried, in unison. "You lovessss ussss, Mother! Do not interfere. We musssst rid the land of the creaturessss!"

Faster than any being on the island, the triplets traveled to their Mother and snatched her up. Allathair wasn't quite quick enough, and was left standing with a piece of torn shift in his hand. Anger built within him, anger he could see mirrored in D'ana's eyes.

The two had been together for so long, they no longer needed to communicate verbally, and they were gods, after all.

Allathair lowered his head and looked up at D'ana from under his heavy brows. She, in turn, closed her eyes and began chanting in the old tongue.

Sinann and Boann ran off, leaving little trails of water where their tears had touched the ground. Luna hid herself completely behind the clouds as Lugh ducked lower behind the hills, darkness following. Luna tried to follow Lugh, though she dared not go to him for comfort. Everyone knew Lugh had been goading the younger boys on, and he might be the next one punished.

Allathair waited a beat of his heart, then joined the chanting. The triplets hissed and struggled, letting D'ana go free as they thrashed about on the ground. With a final grunting scream, they collapsed at Allathair's feet. No longer were they seven foot tall. No longer did they have the legs of a beast. Now they were on their bellies, wriggling, with no limbs at all.

Allathair picked up the closest triplet, wrapping his hands around the beast's slippery, writhing neck.

"You would rid the island of the creatures living upon it. From now on, you will rid the island of the mice and rats and whatever you can catch and swallow whole. You will have no legs to run, and must slide on your bellies. You will have no teeth to chew, but only fangs with which to hold your food as you swallow.

"You will be as the worm above ground. Man and animal will fear you, and you will be alone. So be it."

With that, Allathair released the creature, and the triplets worked their way through the tall grasses, disappearing into the field. D'ana wrapped her arms around Allathair's generous waist, sheltering her face against his chest as she grieved for her lost children.

Many years later, the three were banished once more, driven into the sea by a mortal man. Perhaps killed, as no one has seen them since. Legend has it that there offspring prosper in many other lands.

Seeing is believing, but I am old and not likely to travel far.

Perhaps you will witness what lies beyond!

# Days, Hours, Minutes, Seconds

I can't remember the last time I heard the house, not really. I used to know; in fact I used to know right down to the very second, but they've been giving me drugs. I can't hear it anymore. I can't feel it, but I can remember it.

*Once, I felt it call to me. I felt it pull me. I felt it.*

No longer, although I haven't actually swallowed the pills for several days, and I bet by bedtime tonight I'll feel it. Perhaps I miss it. Perhaps I long to be in that other place. Perhaps it's all illusion brought to life by my tired and frequently twisted mind. Oh I know I'm sick, don't think I believe I'm sane. I know better.

Even though it's been so long I can't remember the *when*, I can remember *it*. The stairway from first to second floors. The wainscoting just around the corner from the last step; I'd run my hand along the white-painted strip until it reached a snag in the immaculate wood.

The snag *wasn't*, not really. It was a button. If I pushed it at the right time, the lower part of that panel would swing inwards, so I could crawl through into the space between the walls.

Crawl slow and silent, so *they* didn't hear me.

I don't think I ever knew who they were. They were just muttered voices between the walls, causing terror to dance across my spine. I could cross from the house, through *it*, to someplace else. Even to my child-mind, I knew where I was going wasn't possible, that it wasn't part of the house. *It* wasn't that big.

They lived between the walls, the voices that terrified me at twelve and continue to terrify me, even now—even at twenty-five. If they knew I was crossing, crawling so slowly that it seemed a day between the rooms, they'd do horrible things to me.

I saw the remains of more than one child there, between the studs and plaster and lathe walls; if I looked down, I could see them just a foot or so below my scraped knees. No matter how long they'd rested there, the look of complete and utter horror was frozen to their tiny features. They didn't rot, they didn't fall apart. They were just *there*. Dolls, broken and abandoned.

And I was as scared of them as I was of the voices.

Carefully, I would put a hand out, set it down. *Wait.* Bring my knee forward, put it down. *Wait.* Opposite hand, repeat the motions.

The other children moved sometimes. Just their eyes, sometimes their little brows would knit together and it seemed to me that I could hear their silent screams.

One hand out, down, wait. Knee forward, down, wait.

So it went, every night, for so long… I don't know why I went through the little door, I don't know why I crawled between the walls, I don't know why I opened the door to the other side. I know I was scared; scared of myself, scared of what was behind me and scared of what lay in front of me. All the time, scared. And night after night, I did it over and over.

*I* waited on the other side of that door, only it wasn't really me. It was, but not. She looked like me and talked like me, but she could do horrible things. She knew I was scared of her. Her name was Maya.

I once watched as Maya took slivers of wood and slid them into the eyes of a bird she'd trapped. The bird didn't make a noise as the wood pierced its eyes; I hoped it was dead. She asked me if I wanted her to come through the wall and do that to Mother.

It was shameful, but I hesitated before I shook my head. I left her standing at a doorway where the beyond was nothing but blackness. I turned back only once, just as she turned to leave the room we shared; the blackness sucked her in with a noise not unlike that of a straw at the bottom of an empty milkshake glass. The bird was left on the floor, twitching. Not dead. *Silent.*

I hated and loved Maya at the same time.

Together we explored other rooms in the house that stood between. I know you're thinking—*'Between what?'.* I can't tell you that, you'd never understand. The house I went to, the house *she* went to—*it*—it was *between*.

And forever whispering, forever nattering… *the voices.*

The house seemed to breathe around us; light cast crazy shadows on walls that rippled and heaved. In that place, the sun moved differently, faster than it should. Sometimes the house was old... old-fashioned wallpaper hung on walls in rooms with very high ceilings, area rugs covered floors set with period furniture. It was in the old house that we met Joseph.

Joseph looked like Maya and I, sounded like Maya and I—but he was a boy. A frightened boy. Maya pinched him, hard and often. He would scream each time, but he looked at her with such love and admiration. He never walked in front of us or beside us as we explored... he stayed behind. Always behind.

I remember we played Chinese checkers and jacks. I remember we played hopscotch on a grid Maya carved into the wood floor beside the rug in the old house. Joseph was terrified the "nanny lady" would find out, and punish us. Mostly, he worried about the "nanny lady" punishing *him*. For two years, he had me convinced the "nanny lady" was going to get all of us, and maybe do to us what Maya did to the little creatures she captured.

I don't know why I stopped playing with Maya and Joseph, except that suddenly I couldn't stand being with Maya anymore. Maybe it was the way she began touching Joseph. Rubbing her hands across his chest before she pinched him. The look had changed in his eyes too... there was something else there now, something visceral and bloody and *hungry*...

Rather than turning right the next time I went through the wall, I turned left. The children on this side could move much more than just their eyes or their brows, they could reach up and pull at my nightgown, or grab at my wrists and ankles. I shudder thinking about their cold, dead hands on me. I can still feel them, you know. The drugs never did take that away from me.

Still I went on, and with each slow, cautious movement... the voices grew louder. It took twice as long to get to the next hidden door.

The house was the same, but new. Can something be the same, but different at the same time? I walked from room to room, looking for another one like me. I was alone... alone except for the voices.

*Alone...*

Suddenly, being alone terrified me more than the voices. I ran my hands along the walls, looking for the way out. There were no buttons, no release knobs... nothing. I was trapped.

Do you know what it is to be trapped, alone, with dangers all around you? Do you know what it is to be left without hope? I did.

Soon, the voices began whispering my name. I heard them whispering, like dead leaves on a dirt road. I heard their laughter.

I could stay silent no longer.

Just as I began to scream, he was there, covering my mouth with his hand. Gary, he said his name was. He'd come from yet another place, somewhere on the other side of what was the bathroom wall, where his door had been. Gary was... older. He surprised me somewhat, since everyone else—all two of them—had been my age. Had been like me.

Gary was not like me. Not like me at all.

He told me stories of the different houses he'd been to. He said if you are careful, and leave the main house at just the right time, you can visit sometimes nine houses in one night. He said he'd met a lot of people wandering the galleys between the houses. That's what he called the dusty spaces between the walls. *Galleys.*

We had to spend a lot of time together, we two. For whatever reason, neither of us could find our way out, and back to the main house. Back to *it.*

The voices laughed from beyond the walls. Sometimes I thought I heard Mother's laughter mixed in with the bellowing guffaws of a man. Still other times, I heard the soft tittering of an old woman... and it was hers that scared me the worst. Perhaps she was the "nanny lady" come to enact vengeance for the hopscotch grid carved so carefully into the floor. When I whimpered and cried out, Gary held me.

Every time we grew tired, Gary would hold me and tell me of his house, through the bathroom wall and beyond the main house. We'd talk long into the night; the nights were longer and the days shorter, there. If I grew frightened, he held me. If I missed my family, he held me. Gary never seemed to tire or need my help. *Gary* held *me.* And years passed.

I *know* years passed. My hair grew, my breasts grew. Gary... well, he didn't change. Just me. I can't remember needing to eat, or drink, or even urinate. I only remember the shortened days and endless nights, and the nightmares that raged forever. And Gary's arms around me, comforting me, sending me back to sleep.

One night, I slept, dreamless. When I woke, Gary was still holding me, but he was cold. When I moved, his arms fell from around me and thumped to the floor.

I scrambled away from him, staring at his slumped body, swallowing my screams.

Splinters were stuck in his eyes, and a wire dangled from his throat where it had slid through the skin, severing the arteries and veins. But there was no blood.

Gary was dead.

I heard a giggle from the far side of the room, and though I recognized it, knew it was her, I could not turn and welcome Maya back into my life. Not now, *not when she'd killed Gary.*

She didn't wait for me. They both came around in front of me, Joseph appeared from the shadows and took my hair in both his hands. Maya came toward me, looking just as she had the last time I'd laid eyes on her. *She* hadn't grown. When she was close enough, I brought both legs up and kicked her—hard—in the stomach. Hard enough to knock both her, *and* Joseph behind me, off balance. Before Maya fell, she hit me, right between my eyes. Pain radiated from each socket as I stood and ran for the bathroom. *Why is it so dark?*

As I slammed the door behind me, I heard a click. I turned the tiny lock to keep Maya and Joseph from getting to me too quickly, and I felt it.

The door had opened. It was there, right beside the main door, and I'd leaned against it.

Everything slowed to a crawl; it was so dark! Seconds, minutes, hours, *days* seemed to pass while I tried to move through air as thick as cane syrup to get to that little door. It was beginning to close when I reached it. My fingers pinched in the hinges as I felt my way around it, my hand grasping the edges and holding it open while I squeezed through.

At that point I didn't care what lay beyond, as long as it wasn't Maya and Joseph.

I sat, curled and still, in the galley between the walls. I heard nothing from beyond, not even the ever present voices. Just silence. Finally, my nerve began to wane so I forced myself forward, crawling on hands and knees... *hand out, down, wait. Knee forward, down, wait.* The blackness of the galley terrified me, the silence terrified me... but what scared me most of all was emptiness beneath me. No shiny, glaring eyes or knitted brows with frozen screams lay there... in the blackness I could see nothing.

Finally, my right elbow ceased to rub against the lathe and studs, and I felt the walls carefully. Another door, but beyond it was... what? Nothing? So far as I could see there was nothing, not a blessed bit of light reached this corner of the hell I found myself in.

I went ahead anyway.

I am *here* now. I don't miss Maya or Joseph. I sometimes miss Gary and the conversations we had, mostly his voice resonating against my ear as I leaned against his chest. I don't know how long it's been since I visited the house... since I visited *there*... When Mother found me lying in a pool of my own blood, outside my bedroom door, five years after I'd disappeared, she had me locked away. She brought me here. She told me Nanny had paid for me to stay here, at this wonderful institution.

*Nanny?* I didn't remember a nanny in my life; no grandmother, no servant raising me. *Just Mother.* Cold chills raised the hair on my arms. *Caught! Punished!*

The doctor says I'm here *for my own safety.* The doctor says that whatever happened to me, I made sure I would never have to see those horrors again. If only he'd believe me. I didn't take my eyes... Maya got them. *I know Maya got them.*

Days, hours, minutes, seconds. They all pass the same here, in the darkness.

Sometimes I can hear Maya whispering from behind the wall. She wants me to forgive her. She wants me to come back and play with her again. She says "nanny lady" has taken Joseph, and she's all alone.

God save me, I want to go. I want to bring Maya back with me, back to play with the doctors and perhaps even... a little game with Mother.

I felt the wall last night. I found the bubble in the paint. It's not a bubble after all, it's a button. It's calling me...

# Chopped Up Pop

I've been away at college, I thought things were okay back home. Mom always answered the phone, and Dad always seemed happy enough when I talked to him. If they'd shown any indication of things going bad, I would have known. Wouldn't I?

I came home for Christmas last week, and found a bloody mess all over the kitchen, and this note on the table.

> Chopped up Pop, cut a strip from his thigh.
> With eggs and beans I made it fry.
> It wasn't bad, beans, eggs and Dad.
> Wasn't bad, I am so glad.
>
> Love, Mom

# Dead Flower

*(Based on the Cap O'Rushes Fairy Tale)*

A long time ago, longer than any one alive today, a little girl lived with her parents and two older sisters. She was as old as all the fingers on her right hand, and she thought that was very old indeed. Her name was Lily.

Every night, after they'd supped on rich stews and fresh bread, after stories had been told and just as the fire was dying on the hearth, the little girl's father would ask each child how much they loved him.

"Rose, my eldest. How well do you love me?" he asked, drawing the girl into his embrace. With a peck on his cheek, she would reply "I love you as well as you wish, Father."

Satisfied, he would give her a tiny sweet and send her on her way to bed. Then he would turn his eyes on his middle child. "Daisy, my dearest. How well do you love me?" he repeated. Daisy, being a sullen and morose child, refused his embrace. "As well as I must, Father." Again he would be satisfied and offer his child a sweet. Daisy would snatch it up greedily, and trot off to bed without so much as a by-your-leave.

Finally, it was Little Lily's turn. "Little Lily, my lovely. How well do you love me?"

Every other night, she told her father the same thing. Every night, it was "I love you, Father, more than anything else under the sun or below the dirt." This night Lily had decided to tell her father something new.

"Father dearest, I love you more than meat needs salt."

A hush fell over the room. Rose and Daisy stopped fighting over the bedclothes, their mother stood quiet and pale at the table. Finally, Lily's father spoke. "What did you say?"

"I said I love you more than meat needs salt, Father." Lily smiled at her father in her childish innocence, not realizing she'd made him very angry. Very angry, indeed.

"How can you say this to me? Do you not love the man who has fathered you, raised you, clothed and fed you these past five years?" Lily's father stood and grabbed her by the shoulder. She cried out, now realizing she'd made him angry, but not knowing why. She struggled against his grasp, great sobs heaving from her chest.

"Get out of my house, you little monster, and don't you ever step foot across this threshold again!" With that, Lily's father pushed her through the door and slammed it shut behind her.

Poor Little Lily. She had to spend the night in the barn with the cows and sheep. She hid from her father in the morning, when he fed the animals. He didn't leave any food for her, and her tiny tummy was so hungry! Lily tried eating the grain in the manger, but it was dry and tasted of dirt.

As dusk fell her mother came to check on her. She told Lily that she must run away as quickly and as far as she could, that her father was so angry he would never let her back into his house. She gave Lily a crust of bread and a bit of cheese and sent her on her way through the forest.

Once upon a time, there was a beautiful young girl who lived deep in the forest not far from here. She had outgrown her old clothes long ago, and now wore breeches and a shift of woven rushes, with a jaunty cap to go with them. She'd long forgotten her name, but those that saw her in the forest called her 'Cap O'Rushes.' She was friend to many around, not just the animals and other creatures of the forest, but also the dairyman and his children, the shepherdess and her flock and the man who drove the coach to and from the big city miles away.

Everyone loved Cap O'Rushes, and she loved everyone right back.

One morning, she heard the sounds of hooves and coach-wheels on the dirt road, and rushed out to greet her friend the driver. This day, however, another man was driving a smaller coach. He pulled to a stop where Cap stood next to the road. She smiled and bowed, sweeping her cap from her head and letting loose all her blonde curls.

"Why, you're a girl!" exclaimed the young man. Cap only smiled, as she as suddenly shy with the stranger. "Would you like to go for a ride, here with me?"

Cap thought for a moment before nodding, and clambered up beside him. She was very excited; she couldn't remember a time she'd ever ridden in a coach before! They waved to the shepherdess, then to the coach driver as he passed them, heading in the other direction, and they waved to the dairy hands taking the cows in for milking. Quite some time later, Cap realized she didn't know where she was. The young man had driven her straight out of her beloved forest!

"Where are you taking me?" she spoke in her tiny voice. "I don't know where I am!"

"Don't worry, young miss. I'm taking you home with me so you can meet my father, the king. I know he'll find you as strange and wonderful as I do."

Cap wasn't sure she liked this idea, but she stayed and only moments later was in awe as they rounded a bend and a castle came into view. She didn't even notice a child run up to the coach and speak to the driver.

"Good afternoon, my prince. Shall I run ahead and inform the cook you have brought a guest?" At the prince's nod, the boy ran off. By the time the prince brought the coach through the gate to the steps of the castle proper, his father the king and his mother the queen were there, waiting to greet their son and his new friend.

Naturally, Cap O'Rushes won their hearts just as thoroughly and quickly as she had the prince's. She agreed to stay with them and be a companion to the young princesses, as well as the prince, of course.

Several happy years passed. One day, the king declared the prince must be wed, and so they would have a magnificent ball, inviting everyone in the land to attend.

Everyone was happy except the maid who loved the prince with all her dark and evil heart. She knew the prince loved Cap O'Rushes, she knew he would choose the orphan stranger-turned-companion over a lowly maid. And so she plotted.

The night before the ball, the maid volunteered to take Cap O'Rushes a mug of hot tea. Into this tea she slipped the grindings of a dried toadstool from a fairy ring. In fact, the evil maid put enough into the tea to kill not only Cap, but two grown men besides!

Poor Cap, she drank the tea without ever noticing a thing.

In the morning, Cap's body was found tucked into her bed, as though she'd simply fallen asleep. The queen herself washed and dressed Cap in her finest clothes, before having the house guards carry her body to the parlor to await a funeral.

Instead of canceling the ball, the royal family insisted on handing out mourning candles to all in attendance; at midnight they would be lit in honor of poor little Cap O'Rushes.

The ball was a splendid display of royalty and riches, and all who danced were treated to foods and drink the likes of which they'd never seen. Only the evil maid noticed that the prince sulked in a corner, far away from everyone else.

She grinned a very evil grin, indeed.

At a side table sat a sad old man with an even sadder wife. With them sat two frumpy and grumpy young women. The father thought they had come a long way to sit and be ignored by the prince. He was about to go and complain—complaining was his specialty—when quiet settled over the crowd of dancers, spreading to those sitting at the tables.

A young lady had entered the ballroom, one who wasn't supposed to be there.

Cap O'Rushes walked past everyone, ignoring the mumblings and whispers—and gasps from one table in particular—and went straight to the prince. There she curtsied, and held out her hand. The prince rose, smiling for the first time that evening, and led her to dance.

After one dance, the prince bent to one knee to propose. The crowd applauded, but no one noticed that Cap did not speak or smile as she should have.

The prince declared they be married at once, and the priest stepped forward to perform the ceremony. More food was carried into the next room, and the ball became a wedding celebration.

To everyone's consternation, Cap O'Rushes walked to each table and removed each salt cellar, smashing them upon the floor. As she approached the last tables, she began to walk as though she'd had too much drink, and a smell came from her like that of rotting meat. Pieces of her skin and chunks of her hair began falling to the floor, leaving blackened holes that bled pus and viscous fluids to cover her body.

When she stepped to the table where the old man, old woman and their two frumpy daughters sat, she howled. It was not an altogether human howl, it was something else entirely. She snarled at the man, grabbed him by his jowly cheeks and bit his nose off. When she'd swallowed that, ignoring his screams, she bit into his cheek and tore a good mouthful to chew.

When she spoke, her voice was deep and gravelly, not at all like it had once been.

"Needs salt."

# My Beautiful Boy

His views on logic did not interest me. My lack of desire to listen to his ramblings had allowed my brain to wander, and I kept myself amused by mentally ripping the skin from his jowly face.

In fact I didn't hear more than five words during his whole twenty-eight minute monologue. When he asked my thoughts, I'd coo about how wonderful it was, how everyone at the conference tomorrow would find him the most interesting and knowledgeable speaker there.

I glared at the back of his head as he faced the window and gazed out on the rotund piece of rock floating beneath us; my mind saw him floating out there beyond the glass, blood pulling away from his body in little drops to freeze in the lack of atmosphere.

If thumbprint ID wasn't required to open doors in this section of the station, I'd have been gone long since. As it was, he and his cronies watched my every move.

I could not stand his continual droning on and on in that snotty monotone. Fantasies of debris from the launch pad smashing through the window and slicing through his pencil-thin neck, severing that constantly babbling mouth from the body that fed it, energized me. I closed my eyes and savored the details.

The boy wearing a torn shirt and jeans pulled the cart across the deck in front of the small office building. As he trudged it through the door he thought about the rewards he would receive after the hard labor today. Never in his life had he seen so much treasure in one spot; the Outsider would be ecstatic on his return to the compound. No one had found this before, even though it should have been one of the first places they'd searched.

The old floorboards squeaked. He knew they were barely holding his weight combined with that of the cart, let alone the return trip being double that. This would be the final time he crossed the floor in this building, the final time he would have to be frightened for his very life.

Echoes of the past rebounded in the old mine. He had ventured several miles below the surface, seeking the treasure. Whispers of the long-forgotten ocean roared and swirled in the tunnels and caves; a Goddess' cries dying in the dark. The Outsider had once told him that his whole compound was once beach-front property, and that all the sand for miles outside the walls was actually the sea-bed.

The young man couldn't even imagine that much water everywhere. Water was a treasure to be hunted for, just like the precious metals and stones that the Outsider hoarded within the stronghold of the compound.

And he had found a rich supply, the Goddess had blessed him with so much treasure!

Perhaps he could get permission to leave and visit his sisters where they lived on the Station. To leave the dusty rock of existence and visit the sparkling object that hovered just outside of the atmosphere tickled his mind and fired him on. *To leave and do anything, anywhere he chose, even if it was just for a few days.* With all of his hard work, the Outsider was sure to be pleased, and pleasing his Outsider was one of the great joys in his life.

He grimaced slightly as he hefted the giant container onto the cart. Another one, and still another; added to the others he'd removed earlier, that made nine all together. Enough to last the Outsider and the household at least a half-year.

The boy wasn't really a boy after all, as could be seen once he was out of the shadows, under the spotlights. Although small in stature, he was indeed a young man. At least two decades in age, when he stood tall he was only just barely over five and a half feet in height; his build lent to the illusion of youth. Slender but well-muscled, tanned a deep bronze from being out in the sun most of the day, his eyes were a washed out shade of blue as were most of the men.

Too much genetic preferencing in the old days had resulted in men that looked alike: dirty blond, pale blue eyes, short. It had become quite rare to see a man with dark features.

The Raiders, though, they were dark.

He often wondered what it would be like, to be like the Raiders. All well over six feet, dark and muscled like oxen, the

Raiders went from station to station, compound to compound, planet to planet, trading, selling and thieving whenever they had a chance. Raiders didn't believe in a Goddess, *any* Goddess. They didn't even believe in a God. Just themselves.

He thought of the fickle way in which they used the women of the stations and outposts. Often, the women were left with child. On their next trip through the area, if the men remembered which woman he'd been with, he'd visit again. If the child was dark and heavily built, the Raider would take it when he left again. If the child was pale and small, it was left behind. As he himself had been, only to live with the shame his mother reminded him of every day while she was around. She'd even named him *Raize*, a common slang term for Raider. Since the women were not allowed to abandon, sell or give away boy-children, his mother had sold herself into service to an Outsider in order to support her little family and avoid prison.

The next time the Raiders visited, she managed to escape with one, leaving her children behind. The girls had long since left the Rock, seeking their own way in the 'verse.

Leaving Raize behind.

*Oh, blessed silence—finally! How I have longed for your touch.*

I couldn't stop staring at my hands. The blood that had covered them, though having been washed away long since, still seemed to stain the skin. I was sure there were rings of dried gore under the edges of my nails - I was constantly picking at them as though to remove it.

Perhaps no one else would see it. *Could* see it. My bent head only lent validation to my ruse; I was a grieving half-wife, the remaining concubine after the death of my Outsider master. I was finally free at least. Nobody seemed to suspect that I had done him in, I played my part well.

I believed I had everyone convinced that I did in fact love the droning lump of narcissistic flesh that had bought and paid for my services.

There I sat, picking at my nails while the station accountant crunched his numbers. My portion of the assets remaining after the station had taken its chunk could not be reckoned in dollar amounts. Rather, the accountant was telling me I'd be given a set amount to live on, each month, via tix at the station warehouse.

The room we'd lived in for two years had been paid for in full, all amenities included.

*But*, should I show any resistance to staying on the station and continuing my life as his 'widow,' *everything* would be forfeit.

"Madeline, you can have as many lovers or as few, as you choose. You can never marry, and you can never bear a child. Should you wish to leave the station for any length of time beyond that of a months' visit to the City, you forfeit your claim. It will then become station property to do with as the Leaders see fit."

I had a week to make up my mind. I didn't need a week.

I knew what would happen if I returned to the City without a means to support myself. They'd put me back up on the block to be sold as concubine to yet another Outsider. *I didn't want that...*

I wanted to be able to pick and choose my lovers from the wandering, random flocks of human men that I'd seen on the station.

Yes, the chances of my conceiving would be higher with a human, but I'd never had the pleasures of intimacy with one of my own kind. I'd always been for sale to the highest bidder, and those bidders were always Outsiders. Besides, there were ways around conception.

Below, on the human home planet—once lush and green, now an overheated sand dune—there were men who could use that very heat to keep me from conception. There were no codicils stating I could not use sterility as a form of contraception.

I continued to stare at my hands while I considered my position. I was heartily sick of Outsiders, the main tenants of the station. Rarely did humans come and when they did, they didn't stay long. They traded, they drank in the bar, and they left, in a trail of dust and disaster that some Outsider low-rank would then clean up. Even the Raiders didn't stay long here.

If I stayed here, in these rooms where I had finally rid myself of he that owned me, I would be treated as Outsider upper-rank. I could freely walk the station at any time, visiting the bar or docks without reprimand.

I could troll for a human man.

I glanced up at the accountant. For an Outsider, he was actually rather handsome. "Are there any stipulations in regards to birth control?" I smiled as I'd been trained; doe-eyed and innocent, yet the knowledge of the worlds apparent in the slow grin.

"None. He was advised to put one in, but he ignored it, knowing you wouldn't leave the station as long as there were funds at your disposal here."

I nodded. Glancing out the window to my left, I observed the planet of my birth. I could not remember anything other than constant, unforgiving heat searing through the atmosphere and literally baking the surface. The Station was cool, maintained at a constant temperature just below comfortable for humans.

Down there, a hack could burn the lining from my uterus. Anesthesia was no longer an option down there, not for humans. I could live with the pain, so long as I remembered the freedom. It was the *smell* of my own burning flesh that would get to me.

Not to mention the smell on the planet itself. Earth One in the old dog days of summer was not a healthy place. Outsider refuse and bio-waste was barely contained all over the planet. Thus, when it really began to heat up—it *really* began to smell.

I sighed. Freedom and money outweighed the cons.

"I'll stay, but first I must visit Earth One."

It was alright in the end, the Outsider was very kind to him, and didn't do the things he'd heard from others in service. His Outsider was as close to a father as he'd get, and he appreciated the fact. If he didn't love the old guy, he'd have left long ago. Raize was not wearing a mark, he'd not been branded—the Outsider felt that was a ridiculous method of marking property—he was indeed free to go at any time, *Goddess Bless.*

When he really gave thought to it, he knew there was no where to go, except home to the compound. He'd die alone and starving in The City.

Raize trudged along, the return trip taking so much longer than before. The cart had become very heavy, and the sun now beat down with an unrelenting fervor. He stopped momentarily, only long enough to pull on his head-wrap. Sighing heavily, he pulled with all his strength; there was only another kilom to go. He could even see the tower at the compound, in the distance... if he squinted. That sight lifted his spirits a small amount, just enough to get him really moving again.

After an eternity in the sun, his skin was beginning to redden and his lips were chapping. If he could only stop and savor the treasure, it would be enough to bring him relief. But he could not, *would not* disappoint the Outsider in such a rude manner.

Finally, he reached the gates and saw they were closed. A strange hush had settled over the usually bustling common area, and the women inside were keening in their strange voices. Panic flooded his chest and he thrust his fists against the gate itself, rattling the chains. He called out, over and over, until at last someone came to let him in.

"He's gone! He's *left*! He said he would not return to the compound again. He was looking for you, was going to take you with him." The guard looked as though he were smirking, and as the younger man looked up into the other's eyes, he could see the laughter. "You've been left behind, son. You're as buggered as the rest of us now. We'll all die here."

With that, the guard turned and stalked back to the common area, elbowing anyone who got in his way.

Raize picked up the cross-arms of the cart once more, and proceeded to the main house. Here, the other containers sat - now entirely empty and wretched, mangled almost beyond recognition. Putting his head down, he threw his weight into the cross-arms and pulled the cart through and into the house.

It was there that he discovered the reason for the Outsider's quick departure. One of the guards had apparently been caught at the treasure and the Outsider had punished him; drowning the man, holding him still while pouring the treasure into his mouth. The Outsider must have done the damage outside, and in here, during the punishment.

Raize howled in anger—not at the Outsider, but at the guard— he'd spent so much time and energy searching for, finding and bringing home the treasure, the water, from the abandoned mine. Their well had begun to dry, and *they needed this water!* How could the guard have been so stupid? Of course the Outsider would be enraged at the small theft!

In his own rage, he kicked the dead man several times - crushing the nose and smashing the teeth. When his rage was spent, he sat on the stair and began to busy himself with getting a small drink from the remaining water in the receptacle that had been sitting on the table. He didn't bother with a cup, he simply drank straight from the container.

Hate had taken hold of Raize briefly, but he had a handle on it now and would be able to go on about the task at hand. *Goddess forgive his lapse into anger.* He'd have to contact the sheriff. The sheriff could clean this mess up, and get him out of the compound and back to the Outsider within a matter of hours. He presumed the Outsider had left for the station, but he was not about to ask one of the others in the compound for verification. They knew he had been the favored one and would find only too much glee in his having been left behind.

He could hear them singing outside now. It made Raize's heart ache to know they would not be missing the Outsider. He had been so kind to all of those in his service, he had always treated them more than fairly. Disgusted with them all, the young man stood and began to climb the stairs to his rooms. He would need to pack his new clothes if he were to be living on-station.

Within an hour the sheriff had arrived, driving up the dusty trail that served the compound as road. He brought with him a mysterious new object that he shone in the face of the compound guards. They shrieked when the light from the strange lamp struck their faces or any exposed skin. He nodded and continued on, giving everyone there the same treatment. When he approached the house, he was cautious—but Raize stepped out with a friendly greeting, startling him slightly.

When the sheriff shone the light on the young man's face, he wasn't surprised to see there was no reaction. To make sure, he scanned the light over any exposed skin, and finally satisfied... nodded.

"Well, boy, you 'scaped a terrible thing by just a little bit. Don' you drink you none of that water there," he said, pointing to the containers Raize had spent all day retrieving. "That there stuff is from the old mine ain' it? Nope, you don' need to answer me, boy, I know it is. It's bad. It shoulda been dumped, but the folks there were scared it'd get inta the underground system, inta the wells. So they locked it up and I see someone found it. I know'd they did, when you called. When you told me what had happened here, I remembered the last time. No, it wasn' your Outsider what had it happen, it was another. Only, he killed everyone on his compound before he took off to the Station. He couldn' a known that it wouldn' effect everyone.

"You see boy, that water there, it has a chemical in it that makes people crazy for a while. Crazy enough, that they' bite their own tongues off before eating, they' bite the nose right off yer face. They' bite anything—and everything—if it didn' get away."

The sheriff grabbed his radio, and spoke quickly into it. Glancing around, he saw the young man's bags sitting, waiting to go. He shook his head, but Raize insisted. He had to reach the Outsider. *His Outsider.* Finally, after a brief radio conversation, the sheriff gave in. "I take ya as far as town, but then ya gotta go out on your own. I know the Outsider from this compound went on up to the station. I ain't gonna help you get there, you can help yourself. The only thing you can do now is wait and hope he comes back for you."

My body was screaming in agony as the Raider healer pulled the hot iron from my womb. The metal guards placed between my legs did little to keep the soft flesh from burning as well, but I bit down, demanding my mind to stay focused.

I would *not* have a child. I would *not* forfeit my life to squeeze some bastard from my body.

The Raiders gave me what comfort they could as I healed and I paid them well when I left. I stayed at the richest hotel in The City to finish my recuperating, spending many days walking the opulent marketplace with its fake greenery and imported cool air.

It was there I found him. *My beautiful boy…*

Raize was casually strolling the dusty street in the commerce section of The City, when a young woman stopped him to talk. She was very well dressed, but marked. He knew she was in service but he couldn't help himself. He asked if she would like to walk with him.

She regarded him closely for a moment, then smiled. She had a beautiful smile - it lit the day even though the sun was out and beating on the poor, dry ground. The young man felt blessed to be with such a one. *Blessed by the Goddess herself.*

As they strolled, she spoke of herself. Her Outsider was dead, which left her technically free. She could do as she wished, so long as she did not leave the station for more than a month at a time, once a year. She spoke at great length, on Raize's urging, about the station. He so wanted to go, so wanted word of the Outsider. His heart fairly burst when she mentioned having seen him.

"Yes, I recognize you. I know of your Outsider," she brushed his hair from his eyes, making him weak-kneed and vulnerable. She pulled him closer to her, resting his head on her chest where he could hear her heart beating in steady rhythm. Her hand stroked the back of his head, relaxing him before she pushed him away to look in his eyes.

"I will send for you in two weeks. Be ready. I must go back to the station now, or I forfeit everything. I can help you but you must give me this time. Your Outsider needs to stay out of this for now. Do you understand? I have need of you, far more than he does."

Raize had no idea what she was talking about, but he nodded, willing to do whatever it took if only she would hold him again; if only she would touch him again. He longed for her touch. She smiled, and fulfilled the need that fairly glowed in his eyes. She whispered a sweet promise in his ear before she left him, standing alone on the street.

It almost broke my resolve, leaving Raize behind. Those scant few moments I had with him fired a desire within me I'd never felt before. I wanted his touch, his breath, his everything. I left The City, carrying a raging heat to rival the surface nestled between my thighs. I had to find a way to bring that boy to me, and damn his Outsider. I had to make him *mine.*

Days passed and he had no word from his mysterious benefactor. New clothes had been delivered, the likes of which he'd never seen before. Daily baths in hot water with luxurious oils had been ordered, along with the finest of foods. Raize had never been so pampered, so spoiled. He was loving every moment of it, and very soon - forgot all about his desperate need to find the Outsider. *The Goddess had promised she would return.*

It wasn't long before I was dealing with my own troubles. Within weeks of returning from The Rock with full intentions of going back for Raize, the Auditor questioned me. He found out who Raize was and knew how to contact the Outsider the boy sought to return to. Rumors of the illness from the treasure had already overtaken the Station and Raize's Outsider was gone, returning to the home world.

They were terrified I was infected with the illness, after less than six hours with Raize. The doctors dosed me up with preventative drugs to keep me from doing anything rash, like biting off my own tongue; a side-effect of the drugs for some, was truth-telling.

I told *anyone* who would listen that I had killed my Outsider. I told everyone I was sorry.

I had killed my Outsider, yes… but they didn't need to know that, and I worried they would believe me. If I confessed and blamed insanity, would they arrest me? No.

Thankfully, they didn't seem to believe me—and they'd already decided my Outsider had simply died of Overuse. He'd always been quite political, after all. They did, however, believe I'd lost my mind.

*Those last few days down on the Rock had really messed her up*, they all thought. In reality, I'd begun to believe they would find out the truth, and toss me into the fray to be sold to another Outsider.

Another side effect of the drugs they gave me caused me to see things. When I looked in the mirror, I could swear I saw pale blue eyes and shaggy, dirty blond hair. *I had to snap out of this and do as I promised!*

The reflection of the mirror stared back at me. I would have sworn it winked at me. *Raize…*

Raize longed to run away from it all, the novelty of being so highly pampered had worn off. She was trying to seduce him from afar, tempting him with freedom from the Rock. His guilt at forgetting his Outsider nagged at him, like the ticking of hundreds of tiny clocks.

Once again, the fuel in the lamps was low, and he fetched kerosene from the desk in the main entrance to fill as many as he could. The house staff had been ordered away by someone, someone he didn't know. Nevertheless, they had left plenty of supplies. In fact, even if his mystery woman didn't call him to The Station for six months, he'd have plenty to eat, drink and be merry with. But what of the Outsider? Where was he? *Why hadn't he come for his faithful friend?*

After lighting the lamps in his bedroom, Raize set the fuel aside and picked up another of the books that had been sent. He'd been lucky; the Outsider believed in education, and while most servants couldn't do more than sign their name on any papers presented them, he could read - and he could understand what was written. The problem of numbers however, that remained something he couldn't work out. Numbers were just so much scribble in a field of parchment.

The books his benefactress had delivered were odd. Most were reprints of old books found in the old cities. He was sure no one had ever read of riding strange animals with four legs, of wasting water and of breathing in smoke on purpose. He found most of the books distasteful, but having nothing else to do, he read them anyway.

Many of the books spoke of the Goddess, and how one could commune with Her using candles and stones and... and *water!* It was in these books Raize would lose himself for hours on end, before visiting the market to seek out the items mentioned.

Some of the afternoons, time passed quickly and there were moments where Raize wasn't sure if he'd been awake or asleep. His body would suddenly jerk, as though startled from a light sleep, and sometimes he couldn't remember having read the passages where his hands rested. Sometimes the echo of the oceans of the past would sound in his ears, terrifying him. *The voice of the Goddess, calling him softly, would cause chills to raise the flesh on his arms.*

Other days, he would give up on reading entirely, and head out into the streets to wander as he would. In the City, there were many more places to go, and new sights to see; he often felt he could stay tucked up like that forever, and other times the guilt would catch up to him and he longed for nothing more than to be doing something useful, something for the Outsider.

There were times he'd catch a glimpse of an Outsider entering a building, and the familiarity of the gait would give him pause. Too often, he'd charge into the building, thinking it was his Outsider, back from the station to find his wayward servant.

*Each time, he was disappointed.*

On his return to the house early one evening, he found another delivery had arrived in his absence. The crates contained even more food and yet more books. Tucked inside one of the books was a letter from his benefactress. Raize tore open the envelope, knowing in his very soul she had finally found a way to get him passage to the station.

*'Little One,*
*Do not think I have forgotten you.*

*All my love,*
*M."*

The date mark was only a few days from when she had left.

Raize found he had to sit on a stair and ask for the Goddess' patience in order to stem the flow of anger. He was frightened for a moment that his temper might have gotten the better of him; he had been known to release his anger. A fleeting image of the dead guard he'd kicked rose in his mind, he dismissed it as he crumpled the page he held in his hand.

Perhaps she was just leading him on with even more promises of the station and a life there, with her and with the Outsider.

Raize stood and walked out of the door. When he reached the street, he turned left—walking determinedly out of the City and straight into the desert. Several hours later, he leaned against an ancient sign beside a decrepit boardwalk. The words *"Beach Closed: Swim At Own Risk"* were barely visible, the paint long since faded.

He stared out at the vastness of golden-red sand as his rage overcame him. What made him who he was fought to maintain itself, maintain control. And then it was gone.

*Raize* was gone.

A smile not unlike a smirk replaced the angered frown, the eyes were no longer gray, but a deep and burning yellow. The color of sand at sunset.

The color of the endless sands at sunset.

*Seth* returned to The City. When he was finished, he would be the only one left behind.


I kept my head down, my hands folded in my lap, while I waited for my doctor. Too scared to look up, I rocked back and forth, taking comfort in the movement. Every so often, I'd peek from underneath my bangs. I'd glance at the mirror.

The man that looked like my Raize was still there. His face had changed, become older and darker; he was angry with me. His eyes glowed, like a *felinx*.

*I want to wake up.*

*Please Goddess, let me wake up!*

# Through New Bedlam

New Bedlam... a small town in the middle of nowhere with nothing really remarkable to make it stand out amongst the thousands of other small towns. That is, until one goes past the pretty surface and looks right into the heart of the town.

The town itself, depending on when you visit, is roughly three miles in diameter, with a smattering of yard-sites just outside town limits. If you visit after the summer of 2008, you'll see something different.

That's the plus side of visiting the town imagination created. You can pick and choose when you arrive... but there are no guarantees when you can leave.

With its very nature, New Bedlam is different; every resident has a different story, every visitor sees a different façade. No one can be *entirely* positive when New Bedlam was founded, or by whom, or why. We can only go by records left behind, and they are sketchy at best. Even *where* New Bedlam is, is a bit of a mystery; one moment you're on the road to St. Louis to visit friends, and the next you find yourself passing a road sign that says Winnipeg - 20 km.

Cell phones work until the town sign comes into view, and then service just sort of fades away; you'll notice residents have no problem using *their* phones as they walk along the tree-lined streets. They'll even wave to passersby, stopping to chat and pass news of the day.

Not with you, though.

Never with you. They'll smile and look away, nod briefly as they step around and past you. The smile never quite reaches their eyes and the nod is almost imperceptible. These people don't want you here.

Trust me, it's not you, it's them. Outsiders are regarded with suspicion and a faint sense of awe and foreboding. Every time outsiders stop in town, something happens. Something not right, something dark. Something evil.

They say that very evil was brought by an outsider and has permeated the town, but those whose families have been here since the beginning know the evil was here first. They are the guardians, the scales of balance. They'll tell you—if you're even lucky enough to get one to talk to you—the balance they keep is maintained with great difficulty, and only just barely.

A story is told amongst the very oldest that there will come a time that balance will be restored, permanently. The crow and the painted lady will bring the wolf and the child. Together they will cleanse the very earth in preparation for the dark and the light that have shared a single beginning, a united past and move towards a combined future.

I figure it's going to be one hell of a ride when it happens.

If you choose to venture further, please be warned. Everyone sees their reality differently, and everyone has their stories to tell. Watch yourself, that first step can be a doozy.

# Doe Clock Truck

We once talked of walking the streets
Under the lamp post, you in your truck
And I in my tight jeans, fresh from work.

That moment haunts me, nightly.

Your truck, under the lamp post, beneath the clock
Still ticking, still noisy – you were right
Together we thought of stealing the doe.

Would it have given you peace?

The music went on after you switched off, ticking
Bright dancing firelight in your eyes dimmed
No chance for roasted marshmallows or cold beer.

Can you hear their outrage, their tears?

Your truck, through the lamp post, into the clock
Thought of you when it happened, as it happened
Close your eyes and see it now, the doe, the fawn.

Stained with your blood, forever scarred.

# On the Road

It was Dark and Stormy's idea to go back to New Bedlam. Their parents had taken us all there 'on retreat' about five years ago, thinking it would be great for a bunch of college students to see what a real writers community was like. I have to say, I was impressed more with the town, than the people in it. Far more impressed, really. There was something there, something that drew me in and kept me focused for our entire stay.

It was like a voice, whispering in my ear, caressing my very soul with breathy words.

And we're going back to rebuild all that was lost two years ago when that crazy woman set fire to the town. By the time she did, though, most of the residents had allegedly committed suicide, or picked up and left. The whole situation was just unbelievable, and let's be frank here, some of those writers seemed to be dipping into something a little psychedelic, if you get my meaning. Even the stone buildings were gone, according to the aerial and land photos we'd gone over.

*Everything* was gone, except the sewers and some of the pavement on the streets, although Dark said those would be gone by the time we got there. He's a smug bugger, that one, but once he sets his mind to something, it gets done.

The twins—Dark and Stormy—they're the by-product of two well known authors coming together and being creative, probably after a taste of that 'special tea.' Have you guessed their last name yet?

*Knight.*

What kind of freak names their kids something so overly bloody clichéd? Their father himself is such a cliché and their mother is desperate to be different, so they name their kids Dark and Stormy Knight.

Whatever.

So the twins had come into a substantial amount of money and since the county of Lassiter had condemned the collective properties that had so recently been New Bedlam, they made an offer. I guess substantial amount doesn't really cover it. It's safe to say, there are very few fresh college-graduates with this kind of money. The pair of them took us all out to get drunk to celebrate, and while we sobered up the next day, they came up with the idea to rebuild New Bedlam and restore it to its former glory.

Like I said, someone had been dipping into the forbidden mushroom patch.

After four hours in the car, all I wanted was to get out and stretch my legs. Our destination was still a good five or six hours away, and I wasn't sure I could handle much more. Dark was absolutely focused on the road ahead of us, and Stormy was snoring quietly in the back seat. Beside her sat Billi Johnson, her latest fling, whose knee seemed to be rubbing up against Dem Gates' pretty often. Dem is Stormy's on again, off again, and he doesn't seem to mind the constantly fluctuating stream of females that share their bed.

As for me, I only have eyes for Dark, but he only has eyes for the road and the project ahead. I sighed, for the millionth time in the past hour, and watched his lower lip twist a bit.

"I have to pee." I can't resist twisting the knife a bit. I know these miniscule distractions annoy the hell out of him.

"No, you don't. You had one cup of coffee this morning and nothing since. You want me to stop the car so you can get out, walk around, light a fag and contaminate your body further."

"Alright then, I'll pee here." I made a show of undoing the button on my jeans. Glancing over, I saw he was still eyes-to-the-road. "I'll do it, Dark. Watch me."

He knew I wasn't serious, but he did motion to a rest stop just coming into view. It was the most wondrous thing I'd seen in my entire life. After this long in the car, the Gobi desert would have looked welcoming. I reached down to pull my shoes on, and grab my purse. I could feel the car glide over onto the shoulder, then the gravel and finally, as I was tying the laces, we turned and came to a stop.

When I sat up, I caught the look on Dark's face. I turned to see what he was staring at, and felt the world skew sideways under me.

The sign read *Welcome to New Bedlam.*

# Clipped

It was half-past midnight when the paper clips staged the revolution. He looked at the mess on his desk, and couldn't help but wonder what his mother would say, were she alive to see this. She'd probably tell him it was '*revolting, Norman*'. She'd be as revolted as she was revolting; all in all that described his mother to a T. Still though, she'd be right. The mass of sticky, slimy, shiny common office supplies piled on his desk *was* rather revolting. A small 'urping' noise was muffled behind his hand as he forced his rising gorge back to it's original position.

Norman Anderson was a typical cubicle accountant. He'd gone to school with visions of grandeur, of hanging out his shingle in front of his own office after getting his sheepskin from only the finest of colleges. In the end, it was a mediocre college and he'd barely kept it together long enough to graduate.

Now, as he sat in a cubicle in a third floor office, he though he probably could have gone further, if it hadn't have been for the most beautiful woman in the world. Cautiously, he rose out of his chair to peer over the padded wall. He quickly scanned the floor to see if any other workstations had the eerie glow that came from monitors turned on in the dark. *He was safe—he was alone.* He ducked back down.

If you were to decide to stop by and visit Norman, you'd step off the elevator, walk ahead ten steps, and turn right. Walk fifteen more, turn left, then go ahead another ten steps or so, until you reach the mid-office photocopier. Turn right, and a few more steps will finally take you to Norman's cubicle. On this night though, visitors wouldn't need the directions, they could just follow the little trail of paper clips, map pins and staples.

Should one get lost, however, and turn left rather than right at the photocopier, you'd run right into the cubicle belonging to the most beautiful woman in the world; according to Norman at any rate.

Michelle Wanamaker—and didn't *that* bring connotations of all sorts to young Norman's mind—was slender, blonde and quiet. Large glasses adorned her nose, making her eyes look so much larger than they already were. When Michelle smiled, which she did so rarely, a mouthful of silver shone. Where there weren't caps, there were braces. At 28, Michelle had braces.

Norman loved her braces.

In fact, Norman loved Michelle. Even though she was four years his senior, his project manager and she didn't really seem to *see* him at any time, he loved her. He ached for her, low down, deep in his groin. It *burned* until he had to relieve himself between lunch and break every day, in the men's room.

Sitting in his cubicle staring at the mess on his desk, he felt that rising heat again. He glanced towards her much larger cubicle as though expecting her to be standing at the doorway, smiling at him. His fingers snaked around on his desk, seeking some object which when found he popped onto his tongue, then chewed slowly. Taste flooded his mouth; he savored the experience before he swallowed.

Thoughts of the single lunchtime they'd shared drifted around his head.

Across the street, in the rather dirty little diner run by a client of Michelle's. Cheeseburgers, and a shared order of French fries. He'd been so taken by the shine of her braces that he pointed out the lettuce stuck between the wires at her incisor without becoming embarrassed. When she thanked him and smiled again, after cleaning the offending bit of greens from her mouth, he knew he was in love.

And then there was Edgar.

Norman hated Edgar; as much as he loved Michelle, he hated Edgar. Edgar was Michelle's boyfriend, and her boss. Norman knew the private meetings in Edgar's office quite often included Michelle bending to her graceful knees behind the old man's desk. A *'bracing blow'* one of the other guys had commented, standing around the coffee machine two days ago. He'd even gone so far as to jokingly ponder whether old man Edgar's pubic hair stuck in the mass of metal in her mouth.

That made Norman think of the lettuce, caught in the sparkling wires of her braces. He didn't stick around to join in the laughter.

Sitting there staring at the mess on his desk, rousing himself from memories, he felt a justified, righteous anger begin to grow in his mind. Norman would rescue Michelle from the dishonorable grasp with which Edgar held her. He'd *save* her. Again, his fingers traced lightly across the desk, picked up another object which he slid into his mouth. After he'd swallowed, he repeated the motion.

Turning back to his computer, he typed in Edgar's password. He'd already managed to spoof the server into thinking he was actually *at* Edgar's desk. The boss had been such a bad, bad boy. There were some really rather naughty pictures on his little section of the main drive. Little boys, doing some very grown up  things.

Norman's fingers scrambled across the desk, picked up a handful of items and deposited them into his mouth. He smirked, a rather twisted, humorless little smile, as he chewed and swallowed, ignoring the taste of blood as it flooded his mouth. In his excitement, he didn't realize he'd eaten everything in the container and the next time his sought this sustenance, there wouldn't be anything there.

As Norman continued to poke around in Edgar's private material, he discovered something utterly, totally gruesome.

*Michelle.* It had to be Michelle.

The young girl in the photo looked to be maybe fourteen. Just barely beginning to develop, as Norman could see from her pose. The young Michelle held the hand of an older man; although younger than he was now it was very obviously Edgar. On the other side of Edgar was an unsmiling, smart dressed woman who looked like an older version of Michelle.

Norman nearly choked on the remaining bits in his mouth and throat. Was she old man Edgar's *daughter?!?* Scanning through the folder, he found more pictures of Michelle, in various states of undress and rather inelegant poses. *Michelle, his love...*

Images of his love down on her knees, servicing the old man in ways Norman's mother would have said only whores do;

This time, when his stomach contents fought to make a re-appearance he allowed it.

It was half past one in the morning when the map-pins revolted.

Right onto his desk, right on top of the pile of now-congealing paper clips. This time there was more blood, quite a bit more in fact. He didn't feel so good, so he put his head down on his desk.

As he did so a few tears slipped from his eyes. Norman's mouth hurt, and his stomach was cramping. He thought he really should stop this nonsense with office supplies. How could he win Michelle's heart and save her honor if he was still eating this way?

Norman's mind slipped a little further away as he opened the stapler and began to pull the staples out, one by one. If he thought about it hard enough, visualized it strongly enough, the supplies would begin to taste like a cheeseburger. Like the cheeseburgers and fries that he and Michelle had shared at the little greasy spoon across the street. *Michelle…*

They found him the next morning, curled into the fetal position beside his chair. Edgar bent down and tried to pry the stapler from Norman's fingers. Michelle stood with her hands covering her mouth, tears running down her cheeks. Silent, crystal tracks over the pale skin. *How Norman would have loved to watch that.*

Michelle watched as Edgar stood, shaking his head. "He just won't let go of that stapler. I don't understand. And look at this, my love. Look at the mess on his desk. Paper clips, map-pins and staples, and is that… is that blood?" Edgar took the young woman by the elbow, and led her to his office.

There, on Edgar's desk, was a print out of a younger Michelle with younger Edgar, and the unsmiling woman next to them.

*HOW COULD YOU DO THIS TO ME* was scrawled over it in red ink. "How could I do what, and where would Norman have found this picture of us with your mother?"

"I don't know, darling. You used to have it as the wallpaper on your computer, remember? Maybe he found it on the server?" Michelle dabbed at her eyes with a tissue.

"Well if he's found this one, then he found the others too. You know, the ones we took on our cruise." Edgar couldn't help the slightly lascivious grin that spread across his face when Michelle first blanched, then blushed.

"Oh Edgar, what a horrible way to start our tenth anniversary!"

# New Bedlam

*Beginnings*

## Bethlam Hospital
*20 June 1806*

Dr. James Devizes had enough of the arguments amongst his colleagues. For the most part, they were opposed to his current experiment and he was not willing to forsake his goal to honor their wishes, their high-brow morals. He left the hall and returned to his office, ready to pack his papers and return home for what little remained of the evening. As he was about to close the hall door, one of his colleagues accused him of being obsessed with his patients.

He did not believe he was *obsessed* with his patients, he could simply see the reality beyond their madness.

Upon reaching his office, Devizes gathered his papers, guttered the lamp and turned to leave the room. He knew exactly how to proceed. All that remained was to raise the required funds, hire appropriate staff, and convince his family they would be better off in the colonies. His brother had been in New England for some time, and had already expressed an interest in helping establish the experiment.

As he approached the door, he stopped long enough to gaze at the map on the wall. *Yes*, he thought, running his finger along a barely discernible line. When he reached the end, he mumbled aloud: "Right there, that's right."

*I won't take no for an answer. Not from anyone.*

Arabelle Devizes was by no means a weak woman, at least to most, but as she argued with her husband over his plans to move them across the world to a life unknown, she faltered. He could see her will dissolving under his, and knew it would take only one more little push to have her give in to his desire. He had trained her well, learning and exploiting her weaknesses while building upon her strengths.

He took a step forward, set his features and glared down into her eyes. "We are leaving in two months, Arabelle."

Despite the anger in her eyes, despite the tears that rose to trickle across her lightly powdered cheek, she nodded. To reward her, he bent to embrace her and kissed the tear away. "There now, my love, don't take on so. You have nothing left to hold you here. Your friends are among the wives of my trusted colleagues, and I believe they too, are having this very same conversation. You see, darling, I've hired only those I trust implicitly to come along on this journey. You won't be alone." He felt her nod against his chest.

She was little more than another puppet in his life. He had little time to gloat, however, as his children interrupted the moment. The governess escorted all three into the parlor to hear the news of their impending departure.

James Devizes terrified his children. He knew it, Arabelle knew it, and the governess knew it. Not a one of them would look him directly in the eye, and that was how he liked it. *More puppets*, he thought, *they will not argue with me*. Looking at Jamie, he thought perhaps that his son would be the only one to make an attempt at dissension. At sixteen, the boy had begun to live a life of his own, abandoning his studies in favor of pursuing a life in the military. He had his eye on a young lady, the daughter of a captain of the Royal Navy. *Not good enough for the son of Dr. James Devizes.*

Devizes felt the smallest of twinges of guilt as he looked at his son. Perhaps he should allow the boy to stay behind, but he would need all the man-power he could get, and Jamie had not only the strength to handle the patients, he had the experience.

"Children, your mother and I have an announcement to make. You will accept this decision without question, without argument. Is that understood?"

The girls answered with a simultaneous "Yes, Father." Jamie said nothing, only set his jaw further and glared at the wall behind his father.

"Jamie?" Devizes pushed his son verbally, and was mildly amused when the boy met his gaze, anger quietly evident in his stare. "I asked you a question, son, and I expect you to answer."

"Yes, Father, I understand what you've said," Jamie replied. His voice was far stronger than Devizes remembered, deeper, more mature. He wasn't sure, but he thought it might have been at least six months since he'd spoken to his son directly. He nodded.

"Well. I have made the decision to move my experiments and patients to the colonies. We will take as much as we possibly can from the house, but we'll have very limited means to retain a full house staff. You will all be expected to do your share during this transition. I have arranged for your governess to attend us, as well as two of the maids and the cook." Devizes paused to give his words a chance to sink in.

"I won't be leaving with you, Father."

He turned his gaze to Jamie, and waited for the boy to continue. When he did not, he motioned for his wife and the governess to take the girls from the room. Once the door was shut firmly behind them, he stepped closer to his son, and in lower tones, said "I explained this already, boy, I will brook no arguments."

Jamie took a step forward as well, perhaps wishing to have his father back down. This only incensed Devizes further, and he set his feet, preparing for a fight. Jamie stopped at one, however, putting his arms behind his back and standing as though on guard.

"Oh for pity's sake, Jamie, enough with the façade. You are not a soldier yet, and I will not have that attitude under my roof. You are still my son, and I will not be denied by you. You will prepare to leave for the colonies, and you will participate in the establishment of my experiment." Devizes took another small step forward, straightening his back and pulling his shoulders up. He knew intimidation would work to his advantage eventually, but hoped Jamie would show some resistance. *He is becoming a man, after all,* he thought.

He was almost pleasantly surprised when Jamie's demeanor sagged. He'd hoped the boy would give him a bit of a challenge at the very least, but compliance would do far better.

"Yes, Father."

"Excellent, my boy. Now, a young man your age needs a bride, and I suggest we find you one before we leave. I imagine the choice over there is very slim indeed."

"I have already betrothed myself to Lily, Father."

Devizes did not immediately react to the announcement. He took a moment to mull it over, knowing a concession on his part would solidify his stance, but angered nonetheless that his son had made such a poor choice in brides, and without consulting him. Needing further contemplation, he turned toward the sidebar and poured himself a glass of whiskey, swallowing it down without grimace. The burn focused his thoughts once more, and he poured a second glass, then another for himself. Turning, he passed the second glass to Jamie, and smiled.

"Well, then, congratulations, son. I'm sure she will do fine as a wife and mother. Have you spoken to Captain Farrell yet?"

Jamie took the offered glass, sipping at the contents. "No, sir. I have not. I... I was hoping to get your approval before approaching him."

Devizes saw his chance to further ally his son to his cause. "Yes, well, perhaps we should go speak to him together, hmm? I can explain the situation appropriately, and you can speak to your Lily first. Shall we?"

Jamie turned immediately, and headed for the door. He didn't see the smile that spread across his father's face as they left the room.


**Devizes Settlement**
30 June 1809
*Dr. James Devizes Journal*


Four years have passed since I first put forth my posit on exclusionary therapy for the poor souls who resided at Bethlam Hospital, or *Bedlam* as it was called by the common folk. Three have passed since we left London. It seems more a lifetime ago, than just a few short years. Had I but known the fragility of my own dear wife's mind, I would perhaps have taken another road to begin the experiments. At the very least, I would have left her behind to tend the younger children. Arabelle had always been so strong that I never thought she could break, except to my will. Nonetheless, she seems to be rousing from the stupor she has been in, and has begun taking an active role amongst us once more.

Still, I have on occasion been forced to administer the smallest amount of laudanum to quiet her weeping in the dark hours of the night.

Elizabeth has been taken ill, recently. She complains of stomach pain after eating, and shortly afterward will vomit excessively. Before my very eyes, my youngest child is wasting away, and despite all my years in study I have not been able to help her. One of the native women of the area has claimed she can cure Lizzy of what ails her. While I am skeptical, I feel no choice but to allow her a chance to do so. I do not know what I would do without my Elizabeth.

Anne and Jamie are hale and hearty, as is Lily, Jamie's wife. She is well along in her pregnancy now, and should be delivering before the end of the summer. Had I known what skills the girl had before Jamie began his courtship, I would not have been quite so against having her as part of the family. With Arabelle's delicacy, Lily has shown no end of patience, as she has done with the girls. She is always found with the washing, the cooking, the sewing, never slacking or sitting for more than a moment.

The girl is a golden light; I have never been so pleased to have been wrong in my judgment of character.

Holker has taken a bride from among the nursing staff we brought with us from Bethlam. We hired girls who had no family, some of whom were even known to have 'entertained' the gentry from time to time. It is my belief these young women have become quite adept at managing not only the patients but the men on the staff as well. I imagine it won't be much longer before I've heard of more marriages amongst our group. God grant them peace and his blessings, there are none of the clergy among us. Perhaps they are living in sin, but what can we do in the middle of this vast wilderness, two days from the next settlement? We do what we must.

The patients have become much more settled and peaceful since we stopped and set up camp. Before we had the house and office built, when we all still slept in the tents in the yard, I heard the rustling of blankets and clothing in the patient tents. I wonder how many of the staff and the patients have been having affairs while the rest of us are not looking. Soon enough, it won't matter. While we cannot remove the manacles yet, as soon as we have some sort of housing for them, we will. At present they are tethered, much like the livestock. Should the fellows at Bethlam ever know of this, I will be chased from the offices in scandal, yet they keep so many walled up in those cells, like the bears in cages we've seen on our travels.

I took stock of the group this afternoon, and have discovered our numbers down by three. I can account for one loss alone, two others are simply missing at this point, with no one recalling the last time they were seen. For now I won't worry, all of the patients are accounted for and that is the main thing. That is why we are here, after all.

I believe I can turn these miscreant wasters into law-abiding, perfectly sane citizens within the next three years. Time will tell, I suppose.

I feel I must get back to Arthur Holker, however. It was my understanding the man was a confirmed bachelor, and yet within a month of our settling, he approached me for approval, asking that I witness as he and Mary spoke vows to each other. I acquiesced more of curiosity than anything else. Mary is a fine girl, quite a bit younger than Arthur and not as rough as some of the others. I believe she may have been a chambermaid before coming to us. She dotes on Arthur as though he were the sun and moon to her, and I suppose this is as it should be. Arthur himself is no longer as intense and driven as he once was, and I find this to be a most excellent state. He was becoming a bit of a bore. Perhaps it is the feel of warm calves across his back.

I have nothing but the sweetest love for Arabelle, but a man has needs and I must admit to a modicum of jealousy over Arthur's physical happiness. Seeing improvement in Arabelle's state has certainly given me pause to consider approaching her but I must have her well, above my own physical desires.

The girls have become quite taken with Polly, the young Irish girl we hired to work the house for us. When we first approached her in Portland, she laughed us off, speaking her mind outright. She wanted no part of 'wagon-trains and settler ways.' When I explained exactly what it is that we are trying to produce here, she jumped at the chance to join us. I don't know what precisely precipitated her change of heart. It puzzles me still.

She is quite pretty, our Polly. Not yet in her twentieth year, she is old beyond her years. She has told us that her family died on the crossing to America, and her family belongings were plundered by the seamen before they disembarked in New York, leaving her with nothing, and no one. Polly survived on her own without 'lying a-back,' and made her way to Portland where she knew a former neighbor resided.

I don't believe her about not whoring herself out. She is far too worldly for her age. She would make the perfect little courtesan, were this the time and place. Her very smile melts my knees, and I believe fully that she is aware of this. In fact, I'm sure of it; she brushes my fingers every time she passes my tea, she hangs on my every word, and always she *smiles*. I wonder almost daily if she would...

I cannot continue thinking of these things. I am becoming distracted and I would not be so dishonest and uncaring toward Arabelle. I have held to our marriage vows for twenty-five years, and I see no real reason to break them now.

Polly has just come into the room in her dressing gown. I don't know if she realizes I'm here, she seems focused on the fire and warming her toes. Her hair is loose, golden and sleek. I haven't seen it loose since the day we met. I can not fathom the reaction my body has to her; never have I felt this way toward any other woman, not even Arabelle.

*Dear God, save me from this temptress!*

# The Institute

The sun scorched the earth below their feet, and still they walked on. Signs of construction were scattered here and there; a back-hoe, scaffolding, lumber of all shapes and sizes. Jael hadn't expected anything to be there as she'd thought everything was taken in for evidence after first Lee then Andy died on the premises. She knew they weren't accidental deaths, and she believed the sheriff knew as well. They just hadn't been able to prove it. *Well, now we will.*

Johnny stopped fifty yards from the breezeway between the main building and the residences. Jael thought she could see his shoulders stiffen, and she knew his jaw was clenching tight against the emotions he wouldn't allow them to see, couldn't allow them to see. Only she knew what he'd gone through the first time he'd passed through these doors. Only she and Lee, but Lee was gone now.

Lee had died not a handful of feet from where they now stood. She turned and glanced at the spot where his body had fallen, landing twisted, broken and bleeding. Even had there been anyone with him that night, they couldn't have saved him. Almost a year later and still Jael thought she could see stains from his blood covering the gravel of the driveway. She closed her eyes against her imagination, only to find a more detailed scene of her brother's death there.

"So, why did we come out here, anyway? We're not going in there, right?" Isabella asked, breaking the silent anguish of Jael's thoughts.

"I'm with Iz, I am not going in that place. It was bad enough when we came here on field trips in grade school, it's got to be unsafe inside after all these years," Scott replied.

Neither Johnny or Jael spoke, weren't even looking at each other, yet both stepped towards the main doors at the same time, giving their own silent reply to their companions. Jael took the sweater from where she'd tied it around her waist and shrugged it on. Years of exploring old buildings had taught her: the hotter the day, the colder it was inside.

The Institute was a foreboding building. Six floors in height at the main building, with two wings of four floors each, and the adjoined residences with parking lot in front and off to the side. *Such an immense building, and it only housed a hundred patients at any given time,* she thought to herself. *Why would it need to be so massive?* She'd heard the rumors, of course. Conscious patients being forced into experimental surgeries, perfectly sane patients being tortured with electro-shock therapy; her father had once told her that his own mother had endured a week of treatment for what was now known as post-partum depression, and had never fully recovered.

She'd become nothing more than the still, silent woman in the back room, her body nothing more than a husk of living flesh. Jael could remember visiting her grandfather and being taken in to see the old woman in the chair. The back room was an addition off of the kitchen, built by her grandfather specifically to house his legal wife while he played house with her caretaker. Her grandmother stared out the window, gazing forever into a garden of flowers planted by her, but tended by others. When she turned her head to look at Jael, she smiled. *"You're next, dear."*

Jael turned and vomited her morning cereal and coffee on the drive behind her, narrowly missing Iz and Scott as she did so. They jumped out of the way as she heaved again. She straightened, accepting Iz's offer of a bottle of water to rinse her mouth. As she spit the liquid out, she turned her gaze back to the building. She really did not want to go in there, but Johnny had already broken the lock, and was opening the doors. She knew she'd have to show them where Andy's body had been found, she knew she'd have to explain everything, all over again. *Why had Andy come up here alone?* Why had he left her to deal with this alone?

"Come on you all. Time's wasting and I don't want to be here long enough to add another break and enter to my rap sheet. Let's get moving," Johnny barked from door.

Jael nodded and the three of them followed Johnny into the darkness of The Institute, into the heart of the darkness of New Bedlam.

# ꟼnto the Mirror

*Novel Excerpt*

The mirror was leaning against the back wall of the storage room, waiting patiently for someone from the family to come and claim it. Most of the partners and all of the support staff had forgotten it even existed, and those who remembered didn't want anything to do with it.

It *had* to be someone from the family that came for it. It couldn't be anyone else; not a spouse, not an adopted child, not a friend. It had to be one of the five McClane children, their offspring, or one of the 25 grandchildren.

None of those still alive responded to repeated letters and phone calls, and none arrived to claim the long piece of glass in the mahogany frame. It was, at last, the *great*-grandchild of Alec McClane that replied to the old man's lawyer.

Shay had never seen the mirror, and had only memories of listening at the heating grate, hearing bits and pieces of the stories her mother and sister would recall.

Whispers, nothing more.

When the letter arrived, telling her that the last lawyer for the firm was retiring and needed to clean out the rooms above his offices, she found out she was his last resort. The only one left available—or *willing*—to attend to the meeting, Shay felt her curiosity piquing. She had no time to call Jack and it was probably better that she didn't.

He'd only tell her to ignore the letter and let all of Alec's crazy possessions go to some second-hand shop. Since he'd left the *Dhrmin-Grigori*, the Angelic sect responsible for taking on punishments for the sins of humans, he'd become more than very human, he'd become *old*. Maybe not in body, but in mind.

Shay loved Jack Dawes more than anything, even her own life, but actually listening to him wasn't on her list of priorities, and never really had been. Particularly when it came to Grandpa Alec's strange collection of occult crap. No, Jack definitely would not approve.

She left him a detailed note before grabbing her jacket and heading out the door, knowing she would have to deal with the consequences later. Probably a long lecture on fiddling with the occult and getting the DGs down on her again.

Shay bypassed the car for her old Honda Shadow, sliding the helmet over her head with the ease of years of practice. She gunned it on her way down the driveway, easing gracefully into a lean as she rounded the corner.

Nope, Jack was not going to like this one bit.

Allen Baldwin, 80-year-old distinguished senior partner of the Baldwin-Mykalchuk-Baldwin Legal, stood on the balcony outside his office. In all his years, he'd never felt as free as he did after ending the call with Shay McClane. That the girl was coming for her family's collection was not just a relief, it was the culmination of a half-century of legal guardianship over what amounted to rummage sale knick knacks. At least, to the uninitiated eye.

He would finally, *blessedly*, be free of the McClane family. The grin broke into a full smile as he looked down on Main Street. Perhaps the girl would take everything home with her, all of McClane's crap, all of the bad energy, all of the devil's doings. Perhaps it would finally leave New Bedlam in peace.

The street below was full of young people, and why not? It was a beautiful day, the sun shining and only the faintest whisper of a breeze ruffled the leaves. Baldwin closed his eyes and drew in a deep breath, enjoying the scent of New Bedlam's tea roses, now in full bloom. Every street corner had a flower bed, and in each bed grew their world famous roses; startling reds, pinks, yellows and whites, scenting the air with romance.

The bell in the clock-tower above the library sounded once, startling him out of his reverie. It was a passing nuisance, that clock, but no one in town wished to stop it. There just weren't that many working clocks like theirs left in the area, and the woman who ran the library now, she would never hear of it. Even after a century of chiming every hour on the hour, day and night, most folks were still startled when it rang clear at dinner time.

Baldwin knew old Alec McClane was the cause of that. That damn rhyme that drove so many of the old ones mad with fear, crazed with worry over the children's lives. All for the crazy old coot from the mansion, all for his amusement.

*When the bell tolls five*
*The children will die*
*When the bell tolls six*
*Buried with sticks*
*When the bell tolls seven*
*They'll be up in heaven*

Even after all these years, people kept close eye on their kids at dinner time. He felt a shiver go down his spine, a cold he hadn't felt before, standing there in the sun. *Time to have me a nap, wait for that Shay.* Baldwin turned and ducked into his office, away from the sudden chill in the air.

Shay knew the way to New Bedlam like the back of her hand. She'd been there on many trips when she was younger, first with her mother and sister, and then eventually moving there with her aunt.

She couldn't really remember those first trips, but living with Serena she remembered all too well. It wouldn't do to hang around for too long, in case any of Serena's men were still there, alive, looking for more of what Serena could give them.

Shay bore a striking resemblance to her aunt; most of the McClane women looked remarkably alike, except Micheline and Angela, who were blonde. Despite Shay's efforts to the contrary, and much to her embarrassment when she would run across one of Serena's clients, she could have passed for her aunt's twin.

She pulled over to the side of the road, and removed her helmet. Thinking about those years with Serena never did her any good and she'd learned, with help from her mother and Angela, to breathe it out. Every time she felt the past threaten to overwhelm her, she would stop what she was doing, and breathe in measured, counted breaths until the anxiety would pass.

The difference in her personality since she started using her mother's techniques was astonishing. Shay had almost become another person; less angry, less liable to act out in inappropriate ways, less likely to become violent for no real reason. The biggest change in her life though, was Jack. Rather than having to run and find him, or have him hunt her down on Serena's orders, they'd finally affirmed their relationship and with her mother's blessing, began a life together.

In short, she had an *almost* normal life. If it weren't for the regular meetings with the DGs it could almost be Rockwellian.

The tattoo on the side of her neck burned for a moment, then let her be.

*Jack.*

Jack had given her the tattoo as a 'going away' gift, when he thought the *Dhrmin-Grigori* were actually going to kill him for his disobedience. *He may have left the DGs, but he's still using all his tricks on me.* She rubbed the spot absentmindedly, feeling closer to him even through that simple touch. It was meant to be a reminder to her, of his love, a way for her to keep his power after he was gone.

But they hadn't executed him, and the power was split between his tattoo, and hers. When he needed to track her quickly, he could use it.

*If he has to follow me to New Bedlam, if he shows up there,, he's going to kill me,* she thought. New Bedlam was Jack's least favorite place to be. It was a cesspool of negative energy, and the rituals two years ago hadn't really improved anything. The bulk of the nasty was gone, but the residual strands had held on, and multiplied.

Shay had felt it when they'd returned briefly, to bury her mother and aunt, and to say goodbye to her uncles. That longing tension, that sense of being watched, always there. Probably always would be.

She pulled her helmet on, and sped off, trying to gain back the time she'd lost while calming down.

Two hours later, she passed the town limits sign, and eased off the gas a little. She knew where the lawyer's office was, but she was starving and she couldn't resist stopping at Ron's, New Bedlam's first and foremost drive-in.

Ron made the best burgers and fries for a hundred miles around, and they were the two things she craved in the summer months. She'd once tried to convince the man to move to Leary's Mill, but he'd have none of it. "I can't move away from here any more than you could move here, Ms. Shay. My heart is here." Even after the town had been all but leveled, he simply started over, feeding the folks that rebuilt their cursed lives.

The smells wafting from the building had her mouth watering before she had even parked the Shadow. Walking up to the order window, she felt the tattoo tingle again. This time, it was nearly painful, and Shay knew Jack was on his way, and he was *pissed*.

*Damn it, I wish he'd realize I can handle things myself, once in a while.* She doubled her order of fries, as consolation. *Carbing up for a fight, sounds like the old me.*

Without even being asked, Ron himself handed her a small cone swirled six inches high with a combination of vanilla and chocolate soft-serve ice-cream. *The man knows the way to my heart,* she thought to herself, enjoying the moment. She took a seat at a table on the far side of the building, and waited for her number to be called. The ice cream made a small dent in her hunger, but only beef, cheese and greasy fries could really satisfy.

Shay was surprised when Ron carried her food out to her, rather than calling the number. She was only slightly more surprised when he sat down across from her.

"I knew your momma when she was a girl, Ms. Shay. Her sister, too. They were night and day, those two, night and day. I am real sorry about their passing, your momma more than Serena. I know things were hard for you, with her. My son... My son was one of her young men. When he finally came back to us, after being hospitalized, he told us you were there." The big man cleared his throat, obviously uncomfortable in his memories.

"I didn't know, Ms. Shay, or I would have tried to help. I didn't know how bad it was for everyone, until Allen came by last week. He said you might be coming for your grandfather's things. He said you were his last chance, that your uncles hadn't responded to his messages at all."

Shay chewed a fry and watched as Ron tried to find the words he needed, tried to find a way to talk to her. *The man looks like someone hit him in the stomach and his dangly bits all at the same time.*

"Ron, my family is what it is. Angela and I have both made peace with it, and we're moving on. Neither of us is ever planning on staying in New Bedlam long. Believe me, Grandpa Alec's stuff isn't going to keep me here. I'm picking up a few things, and then heading home again. I far prefer Leary's Mills to this..." Shay waved her hand in a sweeping motion, indicating the deceptively picturesque town. "This place."

He studied her for a moment, then nodded and stood to leave. "All right. It's not that we all don't love what your grandfather did for us... before he got sick. Before he taught her... I'm sorry, Ms. Shay, we just don't want one of *her* family here any longer than is necessary."

Shay nodded. "Trust me, I didn't want anything to do with her, dead or alive, and I'm ashamed that I'm related. I worry a lot, like *a lot*, that I'll be like her. Jack and Angela are helping me with that."

"You'll never be like her, Ms. Shay, I know that. I can see it in your eyes. You have a soul. She didn't." Ron patted her shoulder gently, and left her to her meal.

After he was gone, she had a hard time enjoying the burger. It tasted more like the slop her aunt had fed her while she was kept in her room, a drugged prisoner, than the fine grade A Angus beef she knew it was.

Would that woman and her legacy ever just disappear?

Rather than staying at the family estate, Shay booked a room at the New Bedlam Inn. She'd spent enough time in that house of horrors as it was, and until she could face it without a tremor in her spine, she was staying well clear.

After leaving a instructions for an early wake up call, Shay left to head down the street to Baldwin-Mykalchuk-Baldwin. Nothing ever seemed to change on the main drag, except the shops. Every time she returned to New Bedlam, there was a different store trying to make a go of it in the biggest storefront in town, and this visit it was still boarded up. As she examined the lease sign out front, she could tell it had been that way since the rituals.

In one weekend, the *Dhrmin-Grigori* had used her mother, and nearly eradicated the little town, leaving less than a handful of the houses standing, and only the oldest stone buildings of main street fully intact. Their combined efforts created four 'natural' disasters; earthquake, tornado, fire and flood. The combination was what banished the main bulk of the nasty energy in the small town, the energy that sucked the life—and the monsters—from the imaginations of the community of writers. The fire killed Serena, and in a misbegotten attempt to save her sister's life, the flood had killed Shay's mother.

Shay breathed deep, letting the scent of roses cleanse her memory of that weekend. She turned away from the shop, and ducked down the side-alley to the back door of the lawyer's office; she was late and knew the front door would be locked.

Pushing the buzzer beside the door, she waited impatiently. A sudden urge to leave came over her. Not just leave the lawyer's, but leave town as well. She shook it off, mentally putting up the silvered shield Jack had taught her to raise. Finally the door clicked and she pushed her way in, finding her way through the darkened stairwell with ease.

"You're quite late, Shay. I should have been home and had my dinner long ago." Allen opened his private office door, ushering her inside with a quick glance around the outer office and reception area. "Anyone see you?"

"Of course not. That's one reason I'm late getting here, besides stopping to eat." She pointed to the empty food containers on the desk and raised her eyebrows.

"I grew tired of waiting for you, girl. You certainly are not as punctual as—"

"Yes, I know," Shay interrupted. "Serena demanded a great deal of everyone, usually at the toe of her boot or the end of her whip."

Allen squirmed, flushing. "Well, you're here now, that's all that matters. There are some papers for you to sign, and then of course, I'll take you up to view the items."

Shay sat down, and put her feet up on the lawyer's desk. "I don't think so. I think you'll take me up there first, with a checklist of the items I'm to take, and then I'll sign the papers. I might be young, Allen, but I am by no means stupid."

She watched as the old man's shoulders slumped, realizing that he was not out to double-cross her, but was trying to build the courage to go up the stairs to that room. "It's that bad, is it?" she asked, voice softening.

"Did you bring Jack with you?"

"Wow. Okay, no I didn't, but I think he's on his way. Do you want to wait until he gets here to do this?" She brought her feet down, and leaned forward in the chair, resting her elbows on her knees.

For the first time since she'd known him, which really was all of her life, Allen Baldwin looked like he might cry in relief. Her tough girl shell crumbled a bit, and she reached out for his hand. "Okay, we'll wait."

Jack Dawes never drove the speed limit. The glove box was filled with various slips of paper all citing his speed and the price he would have to pay. Eventually, someone would actually toss his ass in jail for unpaid tickets, but in the meantime, he would not drive fifty-five.

As he passed the New Bedlam sign, he glanced at the speedometer. He was only twenty miles over the limit, and with no cops in sight, he pushed the old car a little harder. It was only as he entered town that he applied light pressure on the brake.

The classic Malibu with glass-packed exhaust and Nazareth roiling from the windows eased onto the far end of Main Street with little notice from the pedestrians and other drivers. Despite having been a major player in the near-total destruction of their town two years ago, he and his car were practically unknown. The citizens of New Bedlam just didn't want to know; for most of them, the incident was nothing more than a freak occurrence of nature, a big storm that riled everything up.

Of course, they also ignored every other weird, paranormal and freak accident that happened within the radius of the town. He knew things, things that would curl their souls if they would only believe, but they wouldn't, and he supposed they were safer for it.

Parking across the street from the lawyer's, Jack eased back in his seat, reclining as much as he was able. He didn't think Shay and Baldwin would still be in the office, but he couldn't be sure. He could feel that she'd hidden herself from view. *Damn me, shouldn't have given her that tattoo.*

He decided to wait an hour, to be sure no cleaning staff or other lag-behinds were still present. He planned to get in, find the items the *Dhrmin-Grigori* wanted, and get out. He'd hightail it to the Inn afterwards, curl up with Shay and get some rest before heading back to Leary's Mills.

Movement in the side alley caught his attention, and Jack slid lower in the seat. He watched as Shay and Allen Baldwin shook hands, each then turning and leaving in opposite directions. Neither took notice of the car across the street, he'd worked on that. The DG left him with enough power to work a few spells even Shay couldn't pick up on.

The remnants of power came in handy, but it was a pain in his ass when Shay could use it against him.

He waited a few moments longer, then eased out of the car and quickly crossed the street. He could feel the energy of old Alec McClane oozing from every window, every crack in the masonry. The man was inviting him to proceed, taunting him with his presence. Alec McClane was definitely still attached to his knick knacks.

Jack put his hand on the door, giving it a mental push. Only seconds passed until he heard the click as the locks released, and he entered the building. He knew exactly where he needed to go; four flights of stairs in the main part of the building, and then a small, secreted staircase from Allen Baldwin's office, straight to the storage rooms on the top floor.

One small energetic battle of wills with the remainder of Alec McClane, and Jack found what he was looking for, behind the first door. The old man did not want Jack touching his things, did not want him to turn them over to the *Dhrmin-Grigori*. "You know what, old man? I don't want to be here either, and I don't want to deal with the DG any more than I need to. *You* brought us here, *you* put Shay into this, and that puts *me* into it."

A bang from the back of the room made Jack smile. "I'm not scared of you, Alec, I never was." He moved through the maze created by boxes and trunks filled with little more than trinkets, stopping now and then to put his hand over one or another.

When he'd made his way to the area that the sounds had come from, he could feel it; a dark, leaching sort of energy, trying to pull his power from him. "Ah. You know better, Alec. Your tricks don't work on me, or any other DG—" Jack was interrupted by the clear sound of laughter. Though the hair stood on the back of his neck, it was only a physiological response to the situation. He laughed along with the spirit, albeit a bit more uneasily than he'd hoped.

"It's in here, I know it is." The first thing on the list was an old walking stick, topped with a sterling silver wolf head. In days long gone by, Jack had felt that wolf's bite as the cane struck him at his temple, his old adversary using it to escape capture by the *Dhrmin-Grigori* for some sin left un-repented.

At last, his hand settled on the cold metal, and he pulled it out, speaking of few words of power over it to subdue the energy. "Two more to go."

A jewelry box hidden in a cedar chest, and tucked into a locked trunk proved a little harder to get to. After several moments, just as he was about to give up and bash it in, the lock popped. The ring inside the box needed a tad more effort to subdue, and it nearly wore him out.

Taking a moment to rest, he sensed the spirit's anger hovering in the air. Jack smirked, knowing his relationship with Shay, and previously with Micheline, caused the patriarch no end of spiritual torture. That *he* had been the one to call down the fire on Serena would have, had the senior McClane still been alive, been signing his death warrant. Serena always had been, and now always could be, the man's favorite.

Jack's only regret from that day was in losing Micheline to the water.

Sighing, Jack realized he couldn't feel the final item, even with his energy renewed. A three pound terminated quartz crystal, clear as glass except for a tiny flaw shaped like two lovers; he was certain it was not in the storage room. He knew he'd feel it if it was there. *I'll have to check the house tomorrow, while Shay deals with the rest of this...* *crap*. A boom thundered through the room, echoing in the hallway and stairwell. "Yeah, I get the picture. I'm leaving... but I'm taking your trinkets with me."

# About the Author

***Jodi Lee*** has spent the entirety of her life in the middle of the vast Canadian prairies, where she spends her days as the publisher of Belfire Press, The New Bedlam Project and Needfire Poetry. Her nights are spent in New Bedlam, working on a series of novels based in the fictional town.

Over the years her non-fiction has appeared in *Shroud Magazine*, *Necrotic Tissue*, *The Beltane Papers*, *The Blessed Bee*, *newWitch*, *Noneuclidian Cafe*, and the Michelle Belanger-edited collection, *Vampires – In Their Own Words*.

Currently she and her daughters are working together to create magical reading for new pagan families.

You can visit her at: http://www.jodilee.ca

# New Bedlam
## Town Archives Vol. 1

Edited by
Jodi Lee

**Releasing from Belfire Press - February 2012**
http://www.newbedlam.com

**Releasing throughout 2012 exclusively in ebook format.**

From recipes to ritual, crafts to storytelling, each one is a unique, simple handbook to Sabbat celebrations designed specifically for families new to pagan paths.

http://www.sacredtriskele.net